Praise for Garvan Giltinan

"The cutest, cuddliest body-horror/action-adventure story ever told! I read *Titty Kitties* out loud to my cat. He loved it!"
  —Danger Slater, author of *Impossible James* and *I Will Rot Without You*

"You expect a book called *Titty Kitties* to be weird and hilarious, and it certainly is. Would you expect it to be a fast-paced thriller that even manages to tug at your heartstrings? Read it yourself and find out. Giltinan has written the best book I've read about animals popping out of people's nipples."
  —Ben Arzate, author of *Elaine* and *The Story of the Y*

"Giltinan more than highlights Bizarro's gift for taking a throwaway gag and making it something distinctive, strange, and delightful. This will surprise you and make you miss every pet you ever lost, while keeping you hooked with its distinctive voice."
  —Garrett Cook, author of *Crisis Boy*

Garvan Giltinan

Titty Kitties

THICKE & VANEY BOOKS
ST PAUL, MN

Chapter

The first cat appeared from my left tit. I'd been lying in bed, absentmindedly playing with the lad through my Y-fronts, thinking about my wife Bridget in the next room as she snored her arse off like a pig snorting out a nest of feckin truffles. I hadn't made much progress with me knob.

The bare, gray walls (with, naturally, the bloody sacred heart of Jesus staring down at me; because every bloody Irish home must have one) loomed on all sides as I eased into my morning with some gentle stroking. The scratching behind my boobs started the night before and irritated the fuck outta me. I'm not a doctor, which you've no doubt gathered, so I hadn't a clue what was going on. I put it down to an irritating itchy tit. Or nipple to be more accurate.

So. . . one minute, nothing but a prickly feeling and a slight inflammation in the tit area, and the next, in a quick expulsion of pain, a furry head poked through my flabby man breast, yawned, and purred loudly.

I stared like an eejit down at the top of the cat's head. I was about to croak out an exclamation of surprise, somewhere in the deep recesses of my memory, an image came to mind, and a name to my lips.

"Snooze?"

The cat's ears turned at the name.

"Jaysus! Snooze?!"

In the summer of 1981 I was twelve years old and my parents (bless them in that eternal rest) brought home the bright orange ball of kinetic fur from an animal shelter. By the winter of 1982, Snooze was gone. One morning he just never turned up for breakfast. I bawled me eyes out for days. Every morning, I expected Snooze to saunter across the wet lawn in our back garden, climb up on the windowsill, and wait for his breakfast. But he never did. All that remained were orange tufts of hair clinging to Snooze's favorite chair in the living room and a couple of his toenails where he'd clawed the shite out of the armrest when we'd play-fight.

Now, more than thirty years later, Snooze, with the fiery orange fur, slightly slicked with goo from the birth, was home. His head at least.

I found Snooze's sweet spot at the top of his head, just over the eyes, and massaged the fur. A loud purr vibrated through my long lost pet's body and into my own. You know the weird thing? After Snooze came back into the world, I felt no pain. My body accepted this addition. Or condition. Or whatever the fuck.

"Good boy," I said, as tears welled. I'm not an emotional fella, but Snooze's presence burned my eyes, scratching at buried memories.

My next thought: *I have to tell Bridget about this.* The urge to communicate with Bridget in. . . oh, the last twenty-four months, had dissolved slowly. We saw each other daily, but avoided conversations, unless informing each other of things like, "I'll be late home." "We need bog paper." "Flush the feckin toilet, the handle's right feckin there." Stuff like that. Nothing about events or moments in our days. Nothing about the crazy fucked up dreams about lactating leprechauns with magic rainbow semen and inter-dimensional urine puddles after we ate and drank too much cheese whizz and Guinness. She wouldn't have been interested anyway. But this was different. My mobile lay switched off beside my bed. I hated the bloody thing. We both hated talking on our phones. Even Bridget rarely used hers, and then just to talk with her annoying sisters.

With my free hand I pounded as gently as I could on the wall that separated us. There were no pictures on my walls—except Jesus with his heart and head wrapped in thorns—to rattle. Since the separation of rooms and lives—five years gone, now—I'd never bothered putting up pictures or posters.

There were, however, pictures on her side. One of my thumps knocked one loose. I heard the heavy frame hit the floor and the glass shatter. Fuck. I knew I'd pay for that one. Bridget's grunting snore spluttered, then ceased. "What in Christ's feckin name. . . !"

Bridget's Dublin accent came out a little heavy when she first woke. A Southsider by birth, she'd married a Northsider, and adopted the mealy-mouthed elements of my thicker accent. Now she sounded like a real Ballymun native.

Snooze's ears pulled back on hearing Bridget's high pitched barks.

She banged back heavily on the wall. I banged again, but she pounded heavier and stronger. Our sounds were mismatched and vibrated the walls. "What in Jaysus's sake was that? Ya woke me up, ya shitehawk."

Bridget's father used to call me the same thing. Not as a term of endearment.

"Bridget," I said, "ya have to see this."

"I told ya before, I'm not gonna look at your mickey if you're still attached to it."

"Woman, I don't want to show ya me mickey," I said. "Come here."

I didn't want to move in case I frightened Snooze. I worried he might disappear. Simply my old imagination.

"It better be cancerous or something," she said. "If I'm missin my beauty sleep, there better be a good reason."

At least she'd kept a sense of humor: Cos I'll tell ya. . . not enough sleep in the world. . .

The longest conversation in a week. The last one she'd complained about the scuff marks in the bowl of the toilet and I'd berated her for leaving her granny knickers hanging in the shower curtain. Same old same old. The two of us, back and forth: clawing banter designed to puncture the skin. We'd become experts.

Snooze started to meow. I knew the message, even after all this time: hunger. Me too. I would have to move.

I hopped out of bed. Didn't bother putting on any pants. Toddled out into the cold hallway. In the other room, Bridget mouthed off something about me being an arsehole.

Snooze tried to turn his head left and right, attempting to meow up into my face. Where was the rest of him?

The plaintive cry came again.

I was about to head downstairs to the kitchen, when Bridget stomped out of her bedroom (our old room), bed-head like an atomic mushroom cloud—a natural match for the heat of her mood as she stood before me, her old, flowery dressing gown, pulled tightly to her ample bosom, knuckles white with rage. She reminded me of Mae West, or maybe Shelly Winters in *The Poseidon Adventure*, only Bridget couldn't swim worth shite. She planned to take lessons with me awhile back, before—

"Well?" she said.

Snooze stopped meowing, and turned his attention on Bridget.

She put the fear in me standing there all piss and rage, but I held myself together, and pointed at the cat poking out through my left tit. To be fair, the light in the hall was pretty shite and painted everything a dull sallow. She didn't have her glasses. Still beside her bed, no doubt.

Through her thin nightgown I could still make out the nipples on Bridget's generous but drooping breasts, and got a little hard. It'd been awhile since I'd seen them. Can't remember my last real hard-on, outside my stiffy in the morning.

"What?" She squinted at me, the corners of her eyes like dried gray pebbles.

"Go get your glasses."

Bridget shook her head. Her face as tight as an elephant's puckered arsehole. She stomped back into her bedroom muttering under her breath.

On an impulse, I licked my cat's head. The fur felt velvety and soft on my tongue. You must lick with the fur, not against. I had to twist my neck and head slightly. Snooze helped, angling his head to accommodate. I bathed his scalp. Inside his ears. Along his neck. Snooze kept his eyes closed and purred like a small engine. The vibration pulsed through my chest to my heart. Somewhere deep inside, I felt the rest of his body awaiting my attention. I didn't worry about hairballs.

Bridget clomped back into the hallway; her thick, black framed glasses with milk bottle lenses made her eyes pop like Marty Feldman. I never liked those glasses. They ruined the esthetics of her face. At forty-eight, she looked old and crabby.

"Now," she asked. "What the fuck am I supposed to be lookin at?"

I pointed at Snooze.

Bridget's eyebrows dipped. She put her hands on her hips and squinted, despite the glasses.

Her eyes narrowed. "What in god's name is that?"

She backed away a step, came forward again, straining her eyes.

"A miracle is what it is," I said. "And 'that' has a name. Snooze. I told you about him. He was one of my cats. When I was a young fella."

"What in the living fuck are you talking about?" Bridget said. The curses that issued from this woman's mouth would scare most of the stevedores down the Dublin docks. I used to laugh my arse off listening to her. The woman could be hilarious.

"It's him," I went on. "I can't explain it. I woke up and there he was. Poking through my boob, purring his little head off like he used to do. Always had a big purr."

Bridget inched closer. One finger pushed her bottle lenses closer to her face. "That's some growth or something?"

"Growths this big don't just appear. Growths don't make noise, like this. Listen. He's hungry."

Bridget backed away as I passed her and headed downstairs to the kitchen.

Halfway down, I yelled, "What we have to eat?"

No reply.

In the kitchen, I started opening and closing presses. Snooze's nose twitched, pulling in odors and smells; his belly grumbled somewhere inside me.

Bridget stood at the door of the kitchen and pulled her dressing gown tighter around her form and shivered.

I could see her in the corner of my eye: her mouth set in a bitter line as she watched me. I slammed one press door a little hard. "We don't have anything he can eat."

"Not my fault you didn't do your shopping," she replied. She was right; I never kept my shelves stocked. Always an issue, to be fair. I never planned ahead. A while back she'd told me I'd have to take care of me own shopping. "You fetch for yourself," she'd said. "I'm not your bleedin servant."

In a huff, I'd fired back, "That's fine with me," and promptly went out and bought the most unhealthy food I could think of, just to piss her off. She had the last laugh, because I put on two stone, which I carried around like a bowling ball under my expanding shirts and pants. My drinking buddies down The Goat liked to throw peanuts at my protruding, hairy belly button. With enough drink taken, their game became a lively competition and I became a bit of a joke.

I started in on her side of the kitchen, knowing she'd react.

"Hey," she said. "That's my stuff."

"Come on! Snooze is hungry."

Bridget rubbed the sleepy gunk which always built up in the corners of her eyes, sometimes soft and runny, sometimes crusty and hard.

"That thing can't be real. You need to go see a fuckin doctor."

"Or a vet. He might need his shots."

"Don't act the maggot with me, Mickey McGee. I'm being serious. If my ma—God rest her soul—was here, she'd say this was the work of the devil."

Even as she said it, I could tell she knew it sounded ridiculous. Her ma, dead five years, and a church going country woman, never, ever, commented on something being "the devil's work."

"Really?" I said. "The devil, with all his vast powers of fuckin temptation and corruption, decides to curse me with a titty kitty."

The name just came to me. Stroke of feckin genius.

"I want you to get checked out."

"Why? He doesn't hurt a bit," I said.

"I don't give a shite if it doesn't hurt, I think you need it looked at."

"Ah, so ya do care." Sarcasm came easy to both of us.

"I care that some weird bloody shite has appeared in my house—"

"It's not weird bloody shite, woman, it's Snooze. I told you about Snooze before."

"Yeah, but like from forty years ago. You were a small fella. The cat's dead."

"Not anymore, apparently." I still don't know why I said what I said next. "You're just jealous, is all." I continued searching through the presses. Snooze stretched his head to look above the shelf. "Snooze is a part of me. He's mine. I'm happy. I have him, and you've got nothin."

Bridget's pale blue eyes bore into me. Her meaty hands clenched. I glanced over my shoulder and saw the hurt in her eyes.

I thought about Leo and Molly. Leo and Molly were ours. They held us together. With Leo and Molly we both had something.

Molly (panther black, except for a streak of white dividing the top of her head) loved to sit on laps and eat mashed carrots as a special treat, her green eyes squinched tight, quietly purring her pleasure. Leo, my one-eyed white fur baby who shat outside the box when irritated, could open the fridge with a paw and abscond with the first thing his claw could hook. He'd disappear under our bed (when we shared our bed) and eat his prize, along with whatever dust bunnies lay around. Leo's act of rebellion. Usually Molly dominated and held the alpha position. At night, Leo and Molly sat on the laps of their favored persons, and smacked and bit each other while we watched Sky News. Mostly instigated by Molly, they would eventually settle down, and purr as we stroked and rubbed them into a rumbling calm. Just as everything fell into peace, Molly would get the last smack in. Leo never retaliated. Just too exhausted. At night, they slept curled together, bodies rising and falling in deep slumber.

Bridget fell apart the day we laid Molly to rest. Or incinerated; whatever you rather. Molly reached eighteen years old, and we loved her sixteen of those eighteen. Bridget seemed to drop off the face of the earth when Molly left us. She didn't eat for days and became easily irritated at the slightest thing: leaving the bedroom lamp on after I fell asleep; eating crisps in bed; unconsciously picking her nose at the dinner table. Small things like that. Soon, her quirks bit away at my levels of tolerance. We stopped enjoying each other's company and the thin line of connection slackened over time. Benign neglect.

Bridget grieved and things changed.

Not long after, Leo passed away. He'd acquired a cancerous lump, which the vet monitored until it became no longer viable or humane to keep Leo and his tumor wandering the house. His pain worsened. I couldn't live with that. Bridget suggested we let him go long before I was ready, and that pissed me off. I would make the decision. Not her. "I'll bloody know when it's time," I told her. But I didn't. I came home one evening, and Bridget told me she'd asked the vet to take care of Leo. I wasn't there. I wasn't fucking there and it wasn't fucking fair. Bridget had taken away my last moments with Leo and I hated her for that. In retrospect, she did the right thing.

Leo only reached twelve. He'd lived in our care for eleven of those twelve years. He missed Molly as much as we did.

And I was sundered. I cried for a week whenever thoughts of my furry cyclops thief crossed my mind. Like Snooze from my childhood, and my snow white cat, Finnegan, from my teens, all that remained of Leo were physical reminders: thin wisps of fur lodged in my clothes—our clothes—were the worst and best mementos. Even with the boxed ashes of Leo sitting by my bed (I'd touch my forehead to his wooden resting place at night, mimicking a nighttime ritual he and I performed when he was alive, before I slipped under the covers), I couldn't help but feel that gaping emptiness at the loss of my friend. My snuggle bunny. To fuck with masculinity. The love that dare not speak its name.

•

Bridget and I mourned Leo's passing. She openly. Me, by myself. She suggested we find another cat to fill our couch and laps, but I wasn't ready and saw the idea as callous and unemotional. Our tempers sparked over the slightest criticism. Our bodies separated and we entered different bedrooms. The emotional gap between us went from a thin line to a solid wall. We continued on that path. Neither of us wanted to be the first to suggest sitting down and sorting through the shite. The Irish don't do crap like that. Time goes on, and emotions fester. In the weeds, and neither of us felt like backing up and finding a way out. The Irish like to fucking suffer, and we're pretty single-minded about how we suffer. You want a logical explanation for how relationships either work or simply crumble? Find a bloody therapist. As for the simple suggestion that we part ways? There was no way in fuck she'd move in with of her sisters. Both of her sisters were older and had turned into gossipy old biddies with mouths you could park a double decker bus in. This was our house. Her house. My house. She wasn't going anywhere. And I had nowhere else to go. Both of us were just too bloody stubborn.

So all this started with the deaths of Leo and Molly. Spiraled. Until eventually, it seemed we shared nothing more in common. So Snooze suddenly appearing and me shoving it in her face like I did. . . Well, just one more bruise to press. And yeah, "You're just jealous," and "You've got nothin," were gobshitey and childish things to spit in her face.

"How dare you say that. And fuck you." Bridget's scowl hung from her face like a wet tea towel.

Bridget's press yielded better promises of food. She was livid, her skin tight, coursing red. I'd really ripped through something vital in her; I could hear it in her voice. The tears were coming, moving through her; she wouldn't cry in front of me.

I stepped up on my tiptoes and looked into the shelf. Snooze craned his neck and sniffed the dry air. "Then why haven't we gotten a cat since Leo and Molly left us?"

"I'm not ready," she yelled.

"Well that's not really a feckin' option, now, is it?" I tilted my head to Snooze.

I pulled out a tin of tuna.

Now I violated her territory. "Hey, that's my food. There's no way you're getting any of my stuff."

"It's not for me, is it? It's for Snooze."

"It's not my fault your cat is hungry."

Snooze turned his emerald green eyes on her. Always the charmer. She started to fall in. Then catching herself, her tone curdled again. "Get your own shite."

Tuna. The chicken of the sea. Whatever that meant. I turned it in my hands, looking for something to pull.

"I was gonna have that for dinner," she said.

I yanked open a drawer beside the sink and pulled out a tin opener and started to twist through the top. I knew this would irritate her, claw through her, give her flesh pimples, stoke her irritability. She'd come to hate the sound of tin cans being opened. When she needed to open a tin, on came the radio and she'd listen to Larry Gogan or whoever, so she didn't have to hear the sound.

"No you weren't," I said. "You have about ten tins in there. At least give one to Snooze."

I kept opening the tin.

Snooze grew even more excited with the sound and his mewls increased in pitch the closer I came to opening the prize. He stretched out his little orange neck, his nose twitching as he smelled the food.

Bridget still watched from the doorway. Eyes narrow with skepticism, but curious all the same.

With the tin open, I went straight to the table, placed the tin down, and sat in one of the old kitchen chairs, which creaked under my weight.

Snooze stretched his head toward the open tin. Couldn't quite reach it. I moved my boob closer, so the tin was right under his mouth.

I smiled down on Snooze's head and said, "Come in if you're comin' in."

Bridget tensed, but remained silent. Then disappeared.

The top of Snooze's head smelled clean. But I caught a hint of the grass he used to rub his head in years before.

"Where have ya been?" I asked softly. Of course I didn't expect an answer. That would be weird. I simply wanted Snooze to hear my voice and feel the vibrations.

Bridget came back and stood at the door, sneaking looks. Maybe she wondered how Snooze felt inside my body. Maybe she wondered: did he echo in waves like Molly when she held her close at night? I don't know. I never asked. But I would have wondered the same things.

How did it feel? Obviously, strange. But only initially. I knew, somehow, that Snooze had become a part of me. Not just poking from my tit. I mean, his body had fused with mine. The functions of his body, were somehow, mine. And vice-versa. It did tickle a little on the inside but our innards calmed each other and purred together.

Bridget took a step over the threshold of the kitchen. Moved tentatively, edging closer to the table. Something loosened in her, like the slight unwinding of a knot. I gave her no eye contact, cos that's the kind of guy I was. As she put a hand on the back of a kitchen chair, she scratched her left breast absentmindedly.

Bridget simply watched as Snooze fed.

"Pet him if yah want. He likes to be petted." We made eye contact, and I felt something flip in my stomach. Bridget, the girl I've known for more than 35 years, seemed suffused with wonder and excitement. Then she looked away.

She sat in the chair opposite, her eyes never leaving Snooze's bobbing head.

Cautiously, she reached a shaking hand to my cat's head and gently touched the fur. Snooze halted his snack and looked up at her, closed his eyes and smiled briefly.

Bridget's eyes welled and she pulled her hand away. I could've sworn I heard her heart humming.

She wiped her eyes, then stood and left the kitchen. "I have to get to work."

Work wasn't an issue for me, but I would at some stage have to get to the dole office to pick up my unemployment check. That thought hit me only briefly. When the time came I could sort it out. How hard would it be to hide one cat under a coat for an hour or two?

Snooze purred.

My furry resurrected friend distracted me.

The meowing started again. I knew he wasn't hungry.

I got the urge to use the bathroom, and somehow, I knew, Snooze needed to relieve himself.

In the bathroom, Snooze and I did the business. Our bodies worked in tandem and I could feel the process as his shite shifted through my, our, colon. Somehow, my pet and I were connected, both internally and externally. What was mine was his. I hoped he wouldn't have me mark our territory. The odor of cat urine, especially male, is a bitch to scrub away.

Chapter

That night, Snooze's placid head lay slightly tilted and resting on my left breast as we lay in bed together.

I woke a couple of times with a recurrent throbbing in my right nipple. I knew what was up this time. So me and Snooze waited.

By the next morning, my old cat Finnegan, who helped me through my teenage years, made his entrance into the world. Whoever said the second one is easier than the first is a fucken liar. It took me a few minutes to catch my breath. More of Finnegan's body had emerged than Snooze's. Finnegan's two front legs and paws appeared, playfully batting at the air as I lay on my back. His coat, pure white, except for three black splotches, two small, forming eyes, and one large, an open mouth, stood out on the top of his head. The face of a wailing ghost. Then the hissing started. Finnegan noticed his new roommate—or bodymate—and attempted to claw at poor, defenseless Snooze. Snooze hissed back, his orange head trying to dodge Finnegan's large paws. Finnegan always had a forceful personality. He held a confidence more assertive than any cat I'd ever known.

I wasn't surprised by the aggro, but I was surprised when Finnegan's claw tore into the flabby flesh on the side of my left boob, right next to Snooze's ear. The wound stung for a few seconds, then the pain dissipated. Finnegan made a daring attempt to reach his adopted titty kitty brother and I bore the effects.

"Stop that you two," I said. Both cats stopped, turned their heads, and meowed. Hungry. I swung my legs over the side of the bed until my feet hit the bare, cold wood of the floor. I sat there a second before getting up, just to make sure I didn't get a head rush. I'd taken a faceplant about a year ago after fainting, and smacked my head on the edge of a table. Bridget always commented on how clumsy I could be, even when we were in secondary school together; I'd trip or fall and she'd think it was cute. I was also shite at sports. Any kind of physical activity involving coordination. We tried roller skating once, when it was all the fashion, and I went on my arse every time she let me go solo. I skint elbows and hands, the lot. Bridget said once, she fell in love with my lack of sports talent, and my love of cats.

At the edge of the bed, I rubbed the sleep from my eyes. My soft bulbous belly rested on my thighs. Snooze and Finnegan hung between my legs, mewling with confusion and frustration.

I basked in the joy of my two kitties and the new energy they pumped through me. Alive is what I felt. Happiness came slowly back, like being hydrated from the inside out. My boys were back. It took a few minutes, but they gradually came to terms with their new living arrangements. Leo and Molly were no different when they were introduced. They'd hissed and growled until both realized the other wasn't going nowhere soon. And slowly they learned to respect each other. At times they invaded each other's mutual space, shooting back a hiss or a clawless swipe. Natural. Boundary testing. Bridget and meself tested boundaries. We hissed, but never swiped.

A scream came from Bridget's room, closely followed by the dull thump of her feet hitting the floor, and her door being flung open. She says she didn't fling it open, but she flung it open. Finnegan and Snooze tilted their heads to the sound, ears pulled back.

"What the feck?" But the answer came in seconds, bursting through the door to my semi-darkened bedroom.

Bridget stood in the doorway, her scrubby dressing gown hanging open. I could see her scraggly picnic patch—an old pet name—peeping through the opening.

Three of us on the bed looked up.

"What the fuck is this?" Bridget said, gesticulating to her exposed boobs—her tone, an accusatory cocktail of panic and anger.

I was confused. I soon realized what was wrong with my wife's tits. A sprout of black hair sprung from her left nipple.

Molly protruded from my wife's mammary. Her steel gray head bobbed, her dark black nose twitched, as she tested the air. Like Finnegan, Molly managed to pull a leg through, but just the left one. Bridget's comically contorted puss jerked as Molly pulled herself from Bridget's tits. Bridget now carried her own titty kitty.

Bridget's head tilted and her mouth dropped open as she noticed Finnegan for the first time. "Another one?" she said. Less venom now.

"Bridget, meet Finnegan."

My wife swayed a little like an oak tree. I hoped she wouldn't faint. Molly's piercing meow brought her back.

"What is happening to us?" Bridget screamed.

"Haven't a clue," I said. "I suppose we could look it up on the Internet."

I mentally smacked myself for not thinking of this the day before. When I have a problem, the computer isn't usually the first place I go.

Bridget's eyes narrowed the way they do when I say something stupid. "You think this is something we can find on WebMD?"

'Maybe Wikipedia." I knew the comment would get under her skin. Her eyes narrowed so close I could have planted seeds in the furrows.

"What about work? I have to go to work this morning."

"Stay at home, for fecksake." I said.

"People rely on me."

"You work in a supermarket."

"I'm our only source of income and I have never missed a day."

"Well, love." I hadn't used the word in a long time. "I think today is a day you're gonna miss."

Bridget started to absentmindedly rub her right nipple, her face, then her nipple again.

I knew the signs. Our family would grow in the near future.

Snooze and Finnegan hissed at Molly. Territory is important to cats, and these two, despite their differences, found a common enemy.

To calm them, I stroked Snooze and Finnegan on their heads, and followed with a gentle rubbing of their ears. Once both cats had settled down, I asked, "You okay?"

"Why?" she shot back.

"Only, you know, you're. . ." I gestured to the exposed nipple she scratched. I knew it wasn't appropriate, but I'd gotten a little turned on.

Bridget realized where her hand had drifted and drew away. But I could see on her face she knew what I meant. "Ah, Jaysus. This is mad it is. What're we gonna do?"

"We'll sort it out."

"How? I have a cat growing out of my tit."

"But look at who it is."

Bridget turned her attention to the gray head. Molly purred loudly.

Bridget's eyes softened. She really noticed Molly for the first time. She put her hand tentatively down on Molly's head, then started to massage Molly's sweet spot just behind the ear. Molly closed her eyes and sank into my wife's hand.

Meanwhile, my two renewed their hiss and bat. I put a hand between them. "Now stop actin the maggot, yus two." Moments later they both began plaintively calling for food.

Molly joined in.

Our babies needed food. We could strategize on how to proceed with our titty kitties later. We all needed a bite to eat.

Chapter

We sat on opposite ends of the kitchen table and watched our pets eat their tuna. Bridget gave way on the tuna ownership and allowed Snooze and Finnegan to share a tin.

Despite being able to sit in the same room together for an extended period of time (a record twenty-five minutes), the silence weighed down the air between us.

Maybe the familiar smell of tuna wafting through the kitchen prompted it, but I could see by the softened look on her face that Bridget started to accept Molly back into her life, despite the unusual circumstance of her return. My wife rubbed her hand against her beloved cat as the gray lady worked her way enthusiastically into the Chicken of the Sea.

Once or twice we shared a glance as our cats fed, but looked away when the pressure of our togetherness became too hard to bear.

When Bridget rubbed her nipple, my boxers tightened. The body sure does have a mind of its own. Bridget's body had changed over the years; my body slumped; time and routine changed everything. The effort, less important. Our bodies, less important. The connection loosed with our bodies. We were hollow shells walking around, not understanding how we could fill each other.

After Molly and Leo left us, friends of ours briefly suggested babies. We were in our early forties. 'Science can work miracles,' some of them said. Our cold reactions were enough to shut them down. Bridget and meself complained about the cheek, the audacity of our friends for thinking babies would pull us through, filling the empty space. At least on that front we both agreed. No. Baby babies would never fill our lives. We talked, but mostly complained. Trivial bloody stuff. Then we stopped talking. Then we just stopped.

Bridget didn't go to work that day. Called in sick. She screamed into the phone as she gave her boss the excuse: women's issues. He wasn't happy. But he didn't have a cat growing out of his tits, so his day wasn't going badly. While she talked, I saw her lovingly rub Molly behind the ears. When she finished she asked, "What now?"

"How the fuck should I know?" I replied. That pissed her off. "I hadn't planned for somethin like this, for fucksake." That really pissed her off. Gobshitey again. But both of us were frustrated. Sometimes a mewl comes out in a moment of frustration. So Bridget took herself and Molly upstairs and slammed the bedroom door.

For a few hours I sat in the kitchen, while Snooze and Finnegan played with some string I found in the drawer. As I dangled the string, Snooze tried to bite, while Finnegan, with the physical advantage, batted with his claws. A fight started. I intervened and set some ground rules for civility. They seemed to listen and purr, but I couldn't really tell the goings on in their tiny cat brains.

I started to worry about Bridget. She'd never dealt well with transitions. She hated change. Even back in the day, when we were teenagers, she found it hard to adjust to transformation. Getting

married was a big one. We'd known each for seven years at that stage, so the proposal was inevitable. Still, she took her time making the decision to accept. Proposing to her as we were huddled in the car at a carwash probably wasn't the most romantic of gestures. But still. . . seven years. I was hitting twenty for fucksake. Two of me best mates were married at nineteen, with kids. Then seven days (one for every year) of serious contemplation and no carnal activities, except for the odd tongue kiss and a quick titty feel. Usually the fella had the cold feet and needed his space. On the seventh day she accepted. Even moving from her parent's house into our own place was like pulling teeth. Fear of leaving the familiar. Her ma, when the woman was alive, scared the shit outta me so I would've been outta there quicker than a fart from a rabbit. But Bridget always came around. We both adapted. Even when change meant separation, like those seven long days.

I remember the day I realized we'd stopped touching each other. It felt wrong, but it also felt inevitable. *Lost* was on and I sat on the couch. The air felt empty. Bridget was upstairs. When I wasn't out with the boys, I stayed in my room, while she stayed downstairs and watched missed episodes.

About lunch time I heard her door open and a plaintive meow. The toilet flushed. A few minutes later, she came into the kitchen. Once again she sat at the opposite end of the table. Through her nightgown, I could see her cold, erect nipple pushing through like a little coat hanger. She stoked Molly's head with one hand and put the other on her fleshy bosom. I wondered if she was teasing me.

A hard silence followed, then. "It feels bloody weird, doesn't it? The peeing. I can't tell if it's me who wants to piss or Molly."

"Have ya taken a shite, yet? That feels strange as fuck."

Silence, but for the rumbling of purrs.

Chapter

"We have to do something," Bridget said. "We can't stay here for the rest of our lives."

Molly watched the string that Snooze and Finnegan were playing with, her head following back and forth. Soon she started meowing, her large paws striking out at thin air, attempting to cross the space between Bridget and me.

"I know," I said. "But, yah have to admit, it's nice to have them around."

Bridget shifted in her chair. She looked uncomfortable. "That's not really the point, is it? At some stage we're gonna have to go out in the real world. I'll have to go to work. We'll have to be seen by the neighbours. What about that? I told Francine I'd help with Lizzy's party tomorrow."

Francine and her daughter Lizzy (no husband) were two of the neighbours we could actually stand. Despite Francine's crazy focus on church and God. When she took a few drinks, she became bearable. We arrived at estate ten years ago, and we all believed we'd found a great place to bring up a family. We wanted our portion of the Celtic Tiger, middle class explosion. We found instead we'd bought into a black concrete hole. Those who could afford to sell their places at a fraction of what they paid drifted away. I lost my job as a tiler's assistant. Not much of a job, but a job. Bridget, a secretary at a collapsing computer company, got laid off. The cashier's job at a local supermarket came along and helped. For a while Molly and Leo filled out our family. They brought some kind of balance, some semblance of normalcy. Like the housing boom and a secure job situation, all that disappeared.

Bridget was right about leaving the house. As much as I would've been happy to have food delivered, so we never needed to step outside the door again, I saw her point.

"Can we just say we're feeling sick?" I said.

"Then what? Francine comes around. Wants to know what's up. We're eventually gonna have to show them. . ." She searched for a description.

"Our titty kitties" I said.

"Titty kitties?"

"That's what they are, right? Titty kitties."

"That's a stupid name."

"It's accurate."

"How about. . . nipple cats?"

"I like titty kitties. They're not comin from our nipples."

"She feels like she's coming from my nipples."

"Then you call them nipple cats. I'm sticking with titty kitties."

Bridget stared down at Molly, who continued to intensely follow the string I'd been using to entertain Snooze and Finnegan.

Bridget shifted to the chair beside me, allowing her and Molly to get closer. I held out the string for Molly, and she swiped. Bridget leaned in so Molly's claws could hook the string. Bridget's right breast hung white and inviting. Bridget noticed me noticing. Started to cover herself.

Then she started yelling.

I saw another hairy head push through Bridget's skin, starting to crown.

Bridget's eyes strained wide.

I shot out of my chair, my titty kitties dangling, meeping like little sheep, and knelt down in front of Bridget.

"Take it out," I said, pointing at her right tit. "You can do it."

"What do we do?" she said, as she fanned out her hands like she'd lost control of her motor functions.

I could tell by her face, she wasn't sure of next steps. Neither was I. Should I take hold of her boob, the man who hadn't touched her body in some time, or should she grab the crown and pull the cat out herself? All the other births happened while we slept, so to actually help manually wasn't something we were prepared for.

Bridget's breath grew sharp and focused. In and out, short bursts, like bellows.

Like an idiot I said, "Breathe like they do on the tele when they're having a baby."

I got a glare that could curdle milk.

With a forceful push, the little thing drove through to daylight. As it did, two ears popped through, triumphantly breaching the surface.

Molly watched, her eyes alert, the string forgotten, her panicked meowing coming in sharp bursts.

Snooze and Finnegan, ears back, watched with eyes wide. Somewhere inside me, I could feel fur rising.

I took hold of Leo's head gently in my hand and helped him into the world. He was a little sticky from his journey, like the others, but his head slipped out easy once the nose and whiskers came through. Then one paw and a leg, then half his body came through. Yes, definitely Leo. My tuxedo Leo. His white bib of fur extending from his neck into a point at his chest. My one-eyed Leo. Our little black and white cyclops.

Yes, an awkward, but successful birth.

Bridget sat back in the chair, exhausted.

I got off my knees and sat back. Snooze watched the new arrival with interest, his head tilting side to side. Finnegan preferred the nonchalant and hygienic approach, by licking his paw and combing it across his head. We waited a few more anxious minutes, but Leo came no farther. The excitement ended.

Our family now complete as we'd run out of tits.

In short breaths, Bridget said, "How do we deal with this?"

"I'll think of something," I said. Both of us knew, thinking. . . not my strongest skill

Chapter

"You want me to just put on a big coat?" Bridget stood in the hallway by the bedroom, eyes beady slits, hands on her wide hips.

"Well I can't think of anything else." I held up the large overcoat the Da left to me when he died. Actually the coat he died in.

Bridget stroked Leo and Molly. She kissed Leo's head. Molly snapped at Leo, maybe because he received a little more attention.

Cats are weird like that.

I smiled at Leo, my cat Leo, and felt a little pissed that he wasn't a part of me. Where would I fit him, anyway? I cringed when I thought about the other places Leo could have bloomed. Ears. Nose. I clenched my arse.

No longer embarrassed about her partial nudity, Bridget still had a tinge of frustration. She paced the hall. "This is what you came up with? This took you three hours?"

"Well you think of something, then." Finnegan swiped at the lining of the coat I held and snagged a claw. I helped him untangle. "Maybe we can train them to be quiet while we're outside."

"They're not dogs, for fecksake," she said.

Good point. Dumb idea, I admit.

"We could tranquilize them on the days we want to go out," I said.

Another look that puckered my arse. Withering looks were Bridget's forte, as you are no doubt aware by now.

"Come on, then," I said, still holding up the Da's death coat. "We give this a go and see if it works. We don't have to go far, just around the block, across the field to the chipper van on Seanachaí Road. Sure that's no distance."

I could see by her face she tried to think of a different plan. Nothing.

She reached for the coat and took it by the collar into her beefy hands. "It still smells like your father."

"Spray it with one of those perfumes you have. The vanilla. I like that one." Bridget gave me a strange look. Not angry. Surprised. She spun around and headed into the bedroom. I pulled on another of the Da's coats, (the man was mad for coats) and that smelt a lot worse than Bridget's. Before I turned into my bedroom, I inched forward to peer around Bridget's door. Finnegan and Snooze were quiet but for a soft burble of a purr which floated across the hallway.

I could see her bed, all rumpled. She didn't make it this morning. Interesting. The walls were pretty bare, like mine (she hadn't rehung the picture I'd knocked off earlier: a photo of two cats sunning themselves on some poxy Greek island, and her own Jesus in his thorny crown picture). Usually she liked to have nice things around her, ornaments, knickknacks, items I'd never really gotten used to over the years: that pointless snow globe from Spain—where it rarely snows—the bloody awful shillelagh her ma left her in a will. Shite like that. Items with no real meaning for me but were in my life. Now I could see they were missing. Some of her clothes lay discarded on the floor. Curtains were half pulled so very little light penetrated the room. I thought about saying something but held back. Finnegan and Snooze tilted their heads and sniffed the vanilla infused air wafting from Bridget's room.

Bridget appeared in the doorway, the overcoat, while large—the Da was an epic man—did not drown her, so she could close it over her titties. We'd decided not to wear anything under the coats, except for jeans, so our cats wouldn't be constricted. It would be cold out, but we weren't going far. Bridget didn't look happy. Leo and Molly, however, purred contentedly under the overcoat.

The doorbell rang. We all froze. Bridget reached out, grabbed my elbow, and faced me. Our curious cats popped their heads out of our coats and sniffed the air, both pairs practically nose to nose, bridging the gap between us. Snooze and Molly hissed a little. Again I felt somewhere inside me a reaction of Snooze's body to the emotional alert. Finnegan and Leo meowed long and pathetic like two squeaky coffins. Bridget and I stared down to the hallway, where we could see through the patterned window, an amorphous shape shifting around.

"Is there anyone there?" came a voice. Francine from next door. "The car is in the driveway." Francine's shape bent down to talk through the letterbox. "I hear something in there. Do you have cats or something? I didn't know you'd got cats."

Bridget froze for a moment, eyes wide. Then down to the cats between us, hoping they wouldn't make another noise. Their animosity seemed to have dissipated and they were sniffing each other.

"I'll call back later. I just want to see if we're still on for the party next week? That would be great. If you're not there, I'm sorry for yellin through your letterbox. Have a blessed day." Jaysus, she yammered on about the 'blessed day' this, and the 'Lord go with ya' that. Making up for getting preggers outside of marriage, I suppose. Born again, and all that.

The letterbox flap snapped shut and we heard Francine's front door close. The tension left Bridget's body, her limbs slackened, and her hands left my elbows. The connection of our bodies, however slight, broke. I realized I'd been holding my breath while she held onto me. Between us, Finnegan reached across the divide and proceeded to lick Leo's head. Snooze must've decided he wanted in on the action and proceeded to groom Molly's chin fur.

After a few more moments we pulled away, only to receive some hissy protests from both sides.

•

Down by the front door we stood together. Fair play to Bridget, the vanilla I suggested did the job on the Da's coat. She even gave a quick spray to my coat. The Da never smelt like vanilla. We didn't button the coats all the way because we didn't want to scare the cats.

My nose started to run. A combination of the scent of the perfume and the mustiness of the Da's old coat, I suppose.

Bridget found an old hankie in the pocket of the Da's coat, handed it to me. I wiped my nose. Only after did I realize what I'd done. Bridget sniggered, and her eyes lit up.

Molly and Leo stared across at their new brothers and slow blinked. Turned their heads to look at Bridget and then me.

Bridget rubbed their heads, two handed. "Do ya think they're getting used to each other?"

"They must be. There's less hissing going on. Maybe they're getting used to each other's scent." I buttoned the coat up to just below Snooze and Finnegan's heads. So far so good. They weren't freaking out. "Let's get this over with. If this doesn't work we'll try something else."

Bridget rocked on her feet, back and forth, her palms extra sweaty. I could always tell when the old nerves kicked in.

Chapter

I pointed at Molly and Leo. "How are they doing?"

"Fine for now, but I don't think they'll like the tight space." Bridget tried to both hold the coat closed, but gave Molly and Leo breathing space.

"Just talk to them in a soothing voice, keep that verbal connection going."

Bridget nodded.

"And if this goes arse-ways," I said, "we head straight back here. If we see someone coming toward us: back to the house."

I slowly buttoned up my coat, covering Snooze and Finnegan. They made a little squeak. "It's okay guys. This is going to be okay."

Bridget buttoned the overcoat until Molly and Leo's heads disappeared. Bridget's side meowed more than mine. Bridget pulled the coat away from her bosom and soothed the cats with a humming of "Macusla," a light air she'd loved as a girl. That voice floated like a soft cloud from an age ago, when it settled over me. I found myself smiling.

Bridget's eyes narrowed. "What?"

"Nothing."

When Molly and Leo were calm, I turned the key in the door, and we prepared to meet the world.

The estate appeared deserted. The place sat derelict for some time now, after neighbours evacuated the community. The crescent of houses that made up our part of the estate supported four homes still inhabited, and eight which were dead-to-the-world.

On our left lived Francine and Lizzy. Abandoned by the father. A disastrous relationship from the start, so I'd been told. Not that I gossiped. Bridget on the other hand. She gave me the story a couple of years ago, before communication disintegrated. I did mention Francine became a little bit of a religious freak. I hoped little Lizzy hadn't been swept up in all that god talk.

On the right our neighbour, Marcus; as camp as a row of tents. Marcus ran a successful and apparently crash proof internet company. He owned a boat docked in Bray Harbour. He always brought around a bottle of expensive whiskey for Christmas. Last New Year's Eve he left following a couple of tense and hours in our company. He bravely tried to cheer us up with humorous and saucy stories about his gay friends in Berlin. Poor bastard. Why, with all that money, he remained in our black hole of a half-populated housing estate baffled me.

Gemma Whelan, a young reporter for the *Irish Independent*, lived straight across from us. We didn't often see her. Sometimes I read her column, or watched her live streaming a breaking story. Gossip, her bread and butter. Also easy on the eyes with nice boobs and short skirts.

I looked left and right. Nobody. To our left, a small park with an empty playground sat cold and sulky. The muddy ground was covered in dog poo. No one to clean it up—not even the dog owners who wandered with curiosity into the estate carried their shite away.

Bridget and I walked toward the play area. She just a few steps ahead. "Where we goin?"

"Let's just walk them a bit," I replied. She slowed and we closed the distance between our bodies and our shoulders touched. "Get them used to walking around in the coats."

"This is ridiculous." Bridget's voice trembled as her shoulder touched mine. "A walk in the park's one feckin' thing, but getting through a shift at the supermarket. What am I gonna say when someone asks what's that under my overcoat—which will be a challenge to wear at the cash register. 'Oh, ignore them, they're just my nipple cats.'"

"Titty kitties," I said. "Let's just get through this."

She didn't reply, but I could hear her whisper down to Molly and Leo.

We came to the edge of the park. Still no one around. The dark, bulbous clouds above us were full to bursting, waiting to downpour.

Snooze voiced his concern with a godawful moan. "Just hang in there, there's a good lad," I said. Surprisingly, Finnegan remained the calmer of the two. I just hoped Snooze's crying wouldn't set him off.

At the edge of the playground, Bridget stood beside me, her face etched with worry. She kept her head down against her coat, giving her an extra chin: not a very flattering profile. But I couldn't take my eyes away, and for a moment I saw Bridget's face from secondary school, no extra chins, all bright eyes and soft skin. She thirteen, me the more mature fourteen. The old heart tripped a little. She looked so vulnerable back then, and now.

Bridget shrieked sharply, breaking the image. "The little fucker scratched me."

"Which one?"

"I think, your cat."

"Our cat," I said. "Mostly yours because he's attached to your boob, but. . ."

She looked ready with a prickly comeback, when her coat started to wail loudly and jump frantically. "Jaysus, they're going at it in there. Ouch!"

"I know it isn't Leo, he never started fights."

"Shut the fuck up and help me."

"Back to the house."

Something shifted in my left nipple. Snooze. "What's happening in there, lads?"

Finnegan started to panic now. Perfect. His claws came out and dug into my skin.

Muffled wails. More claw scratching from Finnegan. My two heard the caterwauling from Bridget's tits. I cradled Snooze and Finnegan.

A smattering of rain hit my forehead. Then more. Any second now the heavens were going to open up.

Bridget right behind me, head down.

We were across the road. The front door ahead of us.

Finnegan cried, more annoyed than scared. Snooze screamed loudly.

Behind me, Molly and Leo were hysterical, as they pushed and pulled and scraped inside Bridget's coat.

Nearly at the door.

Lizzy and Francine stepped out onto their small porch, and I came to a dead stop. Finnegan and Snooze continued their insistent banshee screams.

I could've been a museum exhibit I stood so frozen. Except for the cats. They kept doing what cats do.

Bridget broke the moment as she smacked into my back. I fell forward and Bridget screamed. The cats screamed. Francine and Lizzy screamed.

Next door, Marcus stepped out, his eyebrows knit in confusion. He'd shaved his head.

Before I hit the ground, I put an arm out and braced myself on the dividing wall between our house and Francine's.

"Are you okay?" Francine, a dyed blond with a North Dublin accent you could stand a spoon in, asked. "Do I hear cats?"

"Yeah," Bridget snapped, thinking quickly. "We just got them and we're trying to get them settled."

"Let's see," said Lizzy. "Let's see."

Lizzy's nose ran with snot and her face glowed with excitement like someone lit her up with a candle. Her little shorthaired bob gave her the look of a pixie.

I rooted for me keys in the pockets of the coat. "Can't, love, they're very shy. Ahhh!"

Claws again.

"Are we okay, Mick?" Marcus asked, leaning over the wall on the other side.

"We're fine," I said, still fumbling for my keys. "Just out for a walk."

I could see eyebrows raised and questioning looks cast like fishing lines between Francine to Marcus.

"Is that a cat?" Marcus asked.

Lizzy leaned over the wall. "Can I see? It's my birthday, Mickey."

She always called me Mickey, not Mr. McGee.

Francine looked from my coat to Bridget's, which expanded and contracted every which way, muffled witches' shrieks beneath. "How many do you have?" she asked.

"What's happening?"

Every head turned.

Gemma, her shirt untucked, hair short and perfect as ever, toddled across the street with a wine glass. Right at that moment I wanted to curl the fuck up with a beer. "I heard all this screaming."

"Nothing," said Bridget. "We're fine."

"Let me see the kitties!" Lizzy yelled.

I found the keys in my pocket. Pulled them out.

I swear I could feel the blood in my eyes pounding. Bridget started to whisper behind me. "Fuck, fuck, fuck."

Snooze and Finnegan plaintively issued their own sad complaints.

The key wouldn't insert into the lock. A titty kitty fight broke out under my coat, claws and teeth, and it only took one scratch and bite to break skin. Blood drawn, I could tell. Stun like fuck. What happened next happened quickly, a knee jerk reaction on my part. "Jaysus!" I yelled, and pulled open my jacket, exposing my battling titty kitties to the neighbourhood. Finnegan's head, plainly visible now to the world, snapped at Snooze's paw as Snooze swiped at Finnegan's head. Displaced aggression. None of that behavior mattered. Once the Da's coat opened Snooze and Finnegan stopped, and looked up. Their eyes attempted to adjust to the grayish light. Naturally, the heavens opened and sent down sheets of rain. The drops hit Finnegan and Snooze, catching them by surprise, which started a streak of wails to make a banshee shite its pants.

Lizzy and Francine were gobsmacked.

Bridget stood like a stuffed rabbit and stared at Finnegan and Snooze, exposed to the world. She let her hands drop from her coat and Molly and Leo popped out, screaming for release.

Lizzie and Francine squinted at my titty kitties.

Gemma caught on quicker. And out came her mobile phone. We were live. Nothing would ever be the same.

Chapter

Lizzy reached out and rubbed her hand down Snooze's head. He purred, vibrating at her touch. Delight glowed on the little girl's face. "Ma, he's lovely and soft."

Francine's eyes popped and a hand shot to her mouth. "Are they coming out of your body?"

Finnegan's eyes lit up and reached out his paws to Lizzy.

"That's not possible," Francine said. "Christ save us."

What can one say to that?

"Sorry Francine, we have to get outta the rain," I said.

Francine reached and grabbed Lizzy's hand from Finnegan's head. "Mom, he doesn't bite."

Blood trickled down my chest from panicked nails and teeth, so I disagreed with little Lizzy.

Behind me, Marcus stroked Leo and Molly. "That's fuckin weird, that is." Bridget stood frozen as Marcus touched her. "They're real," he said. Rain came down heavier now. "The black and white one only has one eye."

Gemma, as is her second nature, stepped right up. I could see stories turning over in her head. "This is feckin' deadly," she said as she filmed us. "They're real? They are real. Holy mother of jaysus. I'll have ya on the cover of every newspaper in the world by this time tomorrow. They're bloody real, not muppets. How did. . . ? Where did they come from?"

"Gemma," I said, "please. . ."

But she didn't listen. She was live.

From behind, Bridget pushed in closer to me.

Everyone ignored the downpour, just bombarded us with questions. Like we fuckin knew the answers. I heard nothing but a buzz in my ears and heard the cats' cries. The commotion too much now. Our cats were getting overwhelmed. We were overwhelmed.

"It's freezin, Gemma," Bridget said and pulled the coat closed.

"Can we just get into the house, for fecksake," I yelled.

Marcus produced a mobile. Little Lizzy trained hers on us.

I reached back and grabbed Bridget by the arm, found the keyhole with the other hand, turned the lock, and we both fell into the hallway. We looked like idiots all crumpled there on the hallway floor, the cats yowling with distress. I kicked the door closed, and Bridget and me and the cats, lay there staring up at the ceiling, breathing hard.

In that moment, I regretted having a front door made of that thick, yellow glass.

•

Finnegan licked the skin and the bloody wound around my breast. Snooze still looked a little disturbed, his eyes pulled back. On Bridget's side, Molly and Leo licked each other for comfort and alternated with licking their small course tongues against her chin.

"Why the fuck did you open the coat?" Bridget asked.

"One of them bit me," I shot back. "I wasn't feckin planning on people finding out."

"Well they have."

Knocks on the door. Questions hurled. There were only four neighbours out there, but it sounded like four hundred.

"Ya may want to call into work and say you're not coming," I said.

Bridget placed her arms protectively around Leo and Molly. "What are we gonna do?"

"We could just lie here," I replied. "It's actually kinda comfortable."

Bridget rolled to the side and picked herself up. No easy feat in the Da's coat. The banging on the front door continued. My mobile went off. Bridget's mobile started next, so she pulled it from her pocket. I caught her wide-eyed look. "Jaysus. Everyone's gonna know, aren't they?"

My hands stroked both Snooze and Finnegan. "Gemma streamed us live. That means a lot of exposure, yeah. And she's got a lot of followers on that site of hers."

Thank god both our parents were dead.

"It's the tits," Bridget snapped. "I like the girl an' all that, but it's her knockers and that cleavage that draws the crowds."

She was right. Gemma livened up any old story with that rack. She coulda been talking about bogroll, but those boobs displayed a gregarious personality of their own, I'd watch like bogroll never existed prior to her tits informing me.

"That's why you watch, isn't it?" Bridget said and took off into the living room.

There's no answer to that.

I lifted myself from the floor, and slightly pulled back the curtained windows by the front door and saw everyone outside gossiping back and forth. Gemma glanced my way and I immediately let the curtain go.

Then she banged on the door. "Ah, come on, Mickey. Bridget? Come on out."

No way. No fuckin way.

I stayed in the kitchen for about an hour, playing catch the string with my boys, while Bridget watched episodes of *Lost* with Leo and Molly. But I knew neither of us could concentrate.

Then, Bridget yelled, "Ya better have a look at this."

I entered the TV room and the news glowed back at me. She stood with the control in her hand. And there we fuckin were. On a shaky mobile camera, looking more like a pair of shoplifters caught in the act. Watching myself on the tele, I felt the rise of panic as we were exposed all over again. But the more I watched, strangely, the two people on tele, wearing those oversized, ratty looking overcoats, looked foreign to me. Like a news report about some other bloody fucked up couple.

I edged over to the couch and sat on the edge. The tele version of me tried desperately to cover his body and help protect the two screaming cats under his coat. But the cats poked out. Same as the other Bridget, with Leo and Molly. That couple on the screen looked scared. But I could clearly see on the screen the cats protruding from their tits, because Gemma zoomed in to catch the best angle. Bridget and I had just experienced those moments, yet the report footage riveted us.

The cats brought us back and we finally recognized ourselves on the tele. Reality again. I thought of everyone in our family watching this. Me mates in the pub (ex-mates, I suppose), people from secondary school, Bridget's extended family, her pain in the arse sisters, the whole bloody world. At that moment, our mobiles, somewhere upstairs in our bedrooms, were filling up with texts and voicemails from everyone we know and knew.

Bridget stepped slowly backward to the couch. Her knees hit the edge and she dropped into the cushions on the opposite side of the couch from me. Meows went wild, feeding off the tension which radiated from us, as our hearts pumped.

"What do we do?" Bridget said. I didn't answer. What the fuck was I going to say? "Look at my hair," she continued. "It's feckin hideous."

I focused on her hair, until my eyes latched onto my balding head and beer belly. Fuck, I looked old. The camera catches us falling through the door as Gemma stumbles forward to help us. The door slams in her face.

The footage repeated. Streamed. Tweeted. Instagramed. Out there.

Chapter

Over the next three or four hours, the media invaded our lives like bacteria. News vans, photographers, and a shite loada mobile phones attached to anonymous eyes poured into our ghost estate. Heads of strangers bobbed up and down to get a good old gander of our front door.

Bridget petted Leo and Molly until she got slow blinks. Or blink in Leo's case. "I'm not goin out to talk to anyone. It looks madder than a spastic cat out there."

Despite our worry, all four cats were now purring. As if they attempted to keep us calm. Leo raised his head and Bridget kissed his eye. "Good boy," she whispered.

•

On the tele, Gemma, her cleavage working the cameras, stood in front of our house, being interviewed by RTE news. "Yes, they're neighbours of mine. Wonderful people."

While they recorded her, she recorded them recording her.

A microphone came into view. "And how do you explain what we are seeing in the footage you shot? The breast cats. Are they puppets?"

"Titty kitties," I said to the tele.

"Nipple cats," Bridget amended.

Gemma shook her head. "They're real. I heard them purr and meow. They were real, live cats."

"Do you think they will come out and talk to us?" the interviewer asked.

"Good question," Gemma replied with authority. "They'll have to come out eventually for food. But I'll talk to them. They need a friendly face. I think talking to me will help. I'm a friend first. A reporter second." Gemma flashed a smile. She never lowered her mobile.

Francine appeared. Lizzy stood in front of her, smiling at the camera. "I'm a god fearin person. That's not natural," Francine said. She really looked scared. "Like, how is that possible? Are the cats inside them? Is this a kinda plague? Jaysus, Mary, and all the saints, it could be a punishment."

A disembodied voice of the interviewer: "A plague of cats?"

Gemma stayed in the shot.

Lizzy's smile brightened. "They were soft and meowing and the big orange one licked my finger but mom made me wash my hands cos of the cat germs and I want a cat now cos they're soft."

Bridget and I were on opposite ends of the couch. In my left hand I held a soup bowl at chest level. Finnegan and Snooze used their heads to push each other back and forth snapping up the tuna I'd dumped into the bowl. "Easy boys. Share." I still wore the Da's coat, because the heater didn't work (I meant to get someone out to check it, but forgot) and the temperature dropped. In my other hand I held a can of Smithwicks. On the other end, Bridget mirrored me with her dish of fish. Molly and Leo ate quite pleasantly together.

Bridget placed a dish of popcorn between us, and we both dipped in as we watched our house on the TV and Gemma as she chewed through the attention. Bridget chastised me earlier for being lax with my food shopping. She was right. Popcorn and tuna weren't gonna keep us from starvation for long.

•

The knocks on the door persisted. All evening. Gemma kept calling our mobiles and shouting through the mail box, "Come on, you two, you're already famous. There's a bunch of people online claiming it's all special effects and muppets an' shite like that. They'll be laughing on the other side of their arses when they see the cats."

We didn't answer.

•

We tried watching episodes of *Lost* on the DVD player, but the distraction didn't work. We kept turning on the news. And while we weren't the main event that night (a serial killer, Jack the Dicker, was caught after reining months of terror on the streets of Dublin—at least for men—and whose identity shocked the nation), the footage of us flashing our titty kitties to the world and the media exposure which followed, came a really close second. Besides, a couple of days after the Dicker was caught, the media had forgotten him.

The endless cups of tea took their toll. Around 9:00 that evening our bladders were full. I could sense Finnegan and Snooze needed to piss, so I needed to as well. I got up from the couch and felt more than just Finnegan's bladder protest: he, we, needed to take a kitty shit.

Bridget snapped her head away from the tele. "Where ya goin?"

"To the bog," I said.

She looked at Leo and Molly, who seemed to be riveted by the activity of shapes on the TV, and said, "We need to go, too. Hold on a sec."

"I think we're gonna, ya know, drop a plop. Ya really don't want to be there for that."

"I've lived with your smelly shite for thirty feckin years," she replied. I think I can work through a few minutes."

"It'll be more than a few minutes." We still had the *Sunday World* up there, so I was thinking of getting an old read in while I waited.

The living room looked out onto the back garden and not the front of the house. Nevertheless, from where we stood, lights flashed in the hallway through the glass front door and lit up the stairs to the second floor. We were both cold and started to feel a little claustrophobic, and knew the pressure outside pushed in.

"Okay," I said. Leo and Molly's eyes were wide with excitement. In the dimmer light of the room, Leo and Molly appeared to have pulled their bodies free a little more from Bridget's boobs. But I wasn't 100% sure. I left the living room and headed to the stairs. The lights outside and bounced shadows off the wall of the hallway. I looked back at the door.

"We can't stay here forever," I half said to the air.

"I know," Bridget replied. "I'm only burstin for a pee, Mickey. Let me through first, will ya?"

"For fucksake." Finnegan and Snooze sensed the strain in my voice (fuck, they probably felt it in my whole body) and started meowing back and forth at each other. They'd have us piss and shit all over the place if we didn't get upstairs to the bog.

"Just go," I said, and waved up the stairs.

Bridget legged it past me. "Cheers."

I heard the toilet door slam shut.

Finnegan and Snooze were now meowing with more force. We needed to take that shite. Our ass worm inched forward and I could feel mine and their arse muscles as they pushed it forward and pulled it back. Finnegan and Snooze didn't have a litter box anymore, so I knew if Bridget didn't get a move on, they'd just go in my kacks.

A scream tore from the bathroom. I legged it up the rest of the stairs. The toilet door burst open and Bridget stumbled into the hallway. She pulled the Da's coat over Leo and Molly. Their heads fought for a view.

"What the fuck?" I said.

Bridget pointed into the bathroom but kept her eyes on me. "They're takin pictures."

Her voice raged with panic and anger.

"Wha?"

"There's a bloody cameraman at the window."

I stepped past Bridget. Leo and Molly peaked over the top of the coat, screaming. Finnegan and Snooze called back.

Our bathroom window on the second floor looks out into our back garden. We never bothered to put a curtain up because no one could actually see into the toilet. Only now some oily looking twat with long hair and one of them hippy beards held a camera, taking shots through the window. Rain poured down his face, distorting his features. He must've climbed a ladder or shimmied up the drain pipe. Either way. . .

"Jaysus!" I screamed and rushed to the window. Smacked the pane. That caught the fucker off guard and he screamed something fierce. He fell backward. Flailed his arms. Tried to flap through gravity. He managed to keep his balance and grab the top rung of the ladder, which fell back against the side of the house. Before he'd fully recovered, I pushed open the window—he pulled away to avoid being whacked—and let rip on the wanker. "Get the fuck away with ya. This is our feckin bog, ya fuckstick." This time the ladder left the side of the house. Finnegan clawed the air, hissing, in an attempt to reach the intruder. Instead of flapping again, the cameraman took rapid fire photos at the window, with me, like a portrait, framed nicely, my titty kitties exposed. I knew I'd see them in the newspaper or online sooner rather than later. Before the fucker fell to his death, I grabbed the top of the ladder and pulled him back against the sill.

"Thanks, mate," he said. He gawped at Finnegan and Snooze, who were sniffing the air, attempting to get a sense of this new person. Bridget stood in the background and covered herself.

I gave him my hardest look.

The camera still slung around his neck, he focused on my cats. "They're real."

Below I could hear a grumbling mixture of voices, and other cameras flashed in the garden beneath me. I knew we couldn't sit in the house ignoring the chaos outside forever.

"Tell Gemma Whelan I want to see her," I said.

Chapter

"I don't know if I can do this," Bridget mumbled. We stood at our front door and listened to the noise of the world outside. "They'll want to see my nipples."

"Believe me, they won't want to see your nipples. They'll want to see these guys." I pointed to the hairy heads peeking over the collars of our coats. The temperature continued to drop. Luckily the heat from the cats kept our bodies warm. "We're in here less than a day and we're surrounded by this shite. Gemma's little mobile recording's gone feckin viral and we're the newest fad. I'd rather just go out there. Let them take pictures. Have an old interview, and then tell them to feck off."

Bridget pushed her face into Leo and Molly's furry heads. "I'm scared."

Molly and Leo purred, rubbed her chin roughly trying to transfer as much of themselves to her as possible.

"Jaysus," I said. "Ya think I'm not scared?"

•

Gemma pulled open our front door, and stood as the flash of cameras framed her, blinding us. Shouts of questions followed, but once inside she immediately closed the door. She was dolled up for the cameras, and even in the downpour her raincoat hung open and I could see the tops of her boobs. Bridget noticed me noticing and elbowed me.

Gemma shook off the rain from her hair and looked up at us, her phone ever ready.

"Put that thing away," said Bridget. "And put those things away." She pointed at Gemma's cleavage. Gemma glanced down, looked a little embarrassed and pulled her coat closed.

When she glanced up, Gemma looked delighted and excited to see us. And while we knew her as a neighbour, we'd never become neighbours who chatted or socialized on any regular basis. Christmas last she came over and drank half the bottle of Green Spot whiskey with Marcus and staggered home. Marcus not long after staggered next door. We learned how really fuckin ambitious Gemma was, and how she teared up when alcohol has taken. She always said to us, she'd grab any shaggin story, no matter how scandalous or sensational and work the thing 'till it broke. She had no shame about it.

Her coat dripped on the carpet. Behind her, we could hear the crowds of media people yelling, causing a general to do outside.

"Okay," Gemma started, "I'm really sorry about all this. I really am. But I'm a journalist. I saw a story and just went for it."

"Ya never even asked us," Bridget said. "This is a private thing."

She covered Leo and Molly but let their heads pop over the top of the coat.

"Plus they're ruinin the feckin lawn out there," I said. "Not to mention tryin to get photos of Bridget takin a shite."

"Why the fuck would anyone want to see me takin a shite?" Bridget said. "What have ya done to us?"

"Ah, now," Gemma shot back, "this isn't my fault. As I said, I just report what's goin on. You're the ones with. . ."

She hesitated, searching for the word, gesturing like an idiot, pointing to our cats. "We're calling them. . . ?

"Titty kitties," I said.

"Nipple cats," Bridget said back.

Gemma looked really confused. "That's what they're called? Nipple cats?"

"Titty kitties," I quickly put in.

"That's what we're callin them," said Bridget firmly. "Nipple cats."

"I think titty kitties sounds better," Gemma replied.

Bridget wasn't amused. "If you hadn't sent that bloody footage to the world, then we wouldn't be havin this conversation and that shower of nosy fuckers wouldn't be camped outside the door."

Gemma leaned a little closer. "Can I see them? Like properly see them."

"No photos or film," I said.

I opened the coat. Snooze and Finnegan popped their furry heads from cover and looked around. Finnegan's little paws were making needing motions as he looked up at me with his large eyes. Snooze saw Gemma lean in. His ears flattened and twitched back on his head. He hissed. Gemma pulled back quickly. "He's a little overwhelmed right now, so he's a little testy."

She leaned over to see Molly and Leo. "He's only got one eye."

"He always only had one eye," Bridget said. "That's how we found him. We think he got into a few scraps on the streets." We'd never really talked about our cats with the neighbors, so we gave Gemma a little titty kitty history. Technically, we gave her a kitty lesson, pre-titty. But titty kitty history flows better.

I could see Gemma was rarin to record us with her mobile, to prove to the mad world we were real. "So, this is the way it's gonna be," I started, and glanced over to Bridget for her nod of reluctant approval. "You can talk to us, but no one else." Gemma's eyes lit up. "We're still pissed at you for startin this crap. You bolloxed everything up. It's a bloody circus."

"I can make us money outta this bloody circus," Gemma said.

A loaded moment hung suspended between all three of us, while four cats purred. The vibrations cut the silence.

•

We sat in the TV room watching the house on the screen and the loop of us flashing our pussies. Gemma perched on the edge of one of the comfy seats with the tired and ragged 70s style coverings we really needed to change. But first things first.

"I don't understand how. . ." Gemma started, nodding at the cats.

"Us neither," I said. "Just happened."

"Everyone wants to know about you and these little guys. As soon as my film went viral, people went ape shite. I got calls from journalists, Garda, scientists, doctors, cryptozoologists. . ."

"What the fuck are they when they're at home?" Bridget asked.

"They look for bigfoots and shite like that," I said.

Bridget looked confused. "Bigfoots? Things that don't exist?"

"Well these bloody well exist." Gemma nodded at Leo and Molly. "And people want to see them. I'm seeing them and I still don't understand what I'm seeing."

"They're not gonna go away, are they? Them out there." I even sounded tired to myself.

Gemma shook her head.

"Then what are we gonna do?" I asked. "How we gonna make all this money ya talked about?"

Chapter

"We're gonna go out there," Gemma said and Bridget flashed a worried look my way. "I know it's scary. But I'll do the talking." Gemma approached the front door and turned to face us. "They'll want proof, like. That there are cats under there. We go out there and face them."

Snooze slept and drooled on my stomach, while Finnegan licked his paws, but kept a sharp eye on Gemma. My connection to the boys had grown stronger, I could tell when either of them wanted to lick their arse, as if some residual memory of a natural part of their daily experience stalked the back of their minds. I felt connected to their instincts and senses. Sounds and smells got sharper.

"I think we should give the story to them," Gemma went on. "But only a taste. We can get you booked onto radio and tele. And not just here in Ireland, but in England, Europe, the US. The US laps this kinda shite up. Just look at those *National Enquirer* papers. But this'll be for real—and we can charge people for an interview.

I'll. . . we'll set the price and people'll want to pay just to talk to the titty kitty couple. Hey, that kinda rhymes."

"Nipple cats," said Bridget. "It's less fuckin rude. And can we just slow down? Maybe take a day or two and think about things? All this just happened to us. We need to get used to what's happening more than anyone."

Gemma scowled, but pursed her lips tight. Her words came deliberate and controlled. "What if someone else develops these titty kitty thingies? What if someone grows some nipple dogs? Or, I don't know, an arse gorilla."

"What the fuck's an arse gorilla?"

"The point I'm trying to make is," Gemma continued, exasperated. "Who knows if you're the only people that'll experience something like this. Or maybe there's someone else out there in the world right now playing with their boob pussies."

"Titty kitties," I cut in. "Boob pussies doesn't make a licka sense."

Gemma ignored me. "Boobs, pussies, arse monkeys, whatever. Point is, you won't be unique anymore, will ya? The longer we wait, the more the possibility that orifice animals will be a thing."

"I'm pretty confident it's not," I said. Though I wasn't 100% sure. I got distracted by Gemma's shirt and her tits as they pushed against the fabric the more frustrated she got. Bridget copped on and punched me on the arm.

Gemma calmed herself. "I promise you, I will look after the two of you."

"The six of us," Bridget corrected.

"The six of you. Yes, I will be your manager. If you want to go ahead with this, and in the end, I can't force ya into anything, I will make this work for us. Look, I'm being selfish here. I'll admit it. But we can all benefit from this freak of nature, and it is a freak of nature. And let's be honest, what the hell were ya both thinking of doing with these guys?" She pointed to the kitties. "Cos it was only a matter of time before someone found out. And I guarantee, I'm someone who you'll want in your corner to navigate this media. We've known each other for awhile, for fucksake. Do ya really want a stranger beside ya right now?"

Gemma's little spiel started to sink in.

"Oh, bugger," Bridget said, and looked a little uncomfortable.

"What?" Gemma asked .

"Give me a few minutes, we have to use the litter box." Bridget, looked a little embarrassed, but headed upstairs again.

I hoped she meant the bathroom, because we didn't have a litter box.

Chapter

Outside, flashes of light, a barrage of questions, and a beating of rain assaulted us. Gemma fielded the questions, while Bridget and I pushed through the sea of people. For the life of me I can't remember any of the questions hurled at us, but Gemma kept us moving as she threw back answers, a teasing smile on her face. Francine and Marcus stood off to the side, watching the circus. Marcus mouthed "sorry," but the crowd consumed him, even in his own garden. I vaguely remember opening our coats slightly to let the cats peep through. The lights and chaos freaked them out and they huddled together undercover, shaking.

Gemma suggested we don't stay at home, cos the media, meddlers, and general looksees would never leave us alone. All the while, Gemma streamed herself and us live, coming from the house into the world. Under our coats our titty kitties meowed and cried general distress. The noise and atmosphere overwhelmed them and I could feel the tension coming off Bridget in waves, rippling through the wet air. She pressed against me, shoulder to shoulder, head bowed against the incessant rain. No one else paid attention the downpour. The throng wouldn't part at first, but Gemma, in her own brash authority, made them move aside, like the parting of the feckin Red Sea. It was fucken mad it was. If you'da seen all this shite in a movie you'da been thinking there's no way something like this would've happened with such speed. These people think we're freaks. Me, Bridget, Finnegan, Snooze, Leo, and Molly, were just freaks. Wet freaks.

The crowd opened up to reveal a sleek black limo. Gemma beckoned us. "That's our ride." She continued to push the crowd back, screaming, "No comment, no comment. Soon. Soon. No comment." She certainly knew how to tease the media.

She reefed open the back door of the car with one hand. Needed the other for recording. She held the phone high so she could clearly get her face in the thick of the action.

Bridget dived in first. She kept a protective hand over Leo and Molly, now buried deep against her bosom. I followed behind. Gemma hopped in the front of the car with the driver, a fella who looked an awful lot like a chat show host Mark Roach on RTE 2. Turned out it was Mark Roach from RTE 2.

"Get them to the hotel," Gemma said.

Chapter

Gemma gave us a rundown of what she wanted for us. What she wanted for herself. What she wanted from Mark, who turned out to be a bit of a dick. He told us what he wanted for himself, just dictated his agenda. Bridget kept glancing at me like I knew what to say, how to deal with all this shite.

"They're interviewed by me tonight and don't talk to anyone else for a week," Roach said, like we weren't right behind him.

"You get exclusive TV rights to their story. There's papers chomping at the bit to interview my clients."

"Feckin tabloids? I was told—"

"We can stop the car now and forget the whole thing," Gemma snapped off.

Roach soured. "They'll answer my questions. All my questions. That's the deal. You'll get compensated when we've completed the show. The bosses have found the money—and it's a lot of money—for these two." He gestured back at us like we were idiots and couldn't comprehend the shite he spewed.

"No. Money up front," Gemma shot back. "We talked about this. What you have is the first interview with a phenomenon. Two medical anomalies. . ."

"As far as we know."

"What are ya talkin about?" Gemma went up an octave. "When have you ever heard of people with cats growing from their tits? Look, once the interviews with the newspapers are done they're all yours."

Gemma leaned over the back of the passenger seat, her mobile flashlight blinding the fuck outta me and Bridget and the cats. "We have *The Sun, The Mirror,* and we'll have a few more lined up before you know it, waiting at the hotel for interviews. A lot of money, guys. Especially from the tabs. For once they'll have a headline like 'Woman has Cat Tits' and it won't be bullshite."

"Nipple cats," Bridget said.

"Titty kitties," I cut in. Only to get the stare from Bridget.

Gemma shrugged. "Whatever we call them, we'll have people eating out of our hands." Bridget and I were overwhelmed and it showed in our faces. "I'll look after you guys," Gemma continued. Her face softened. "I promise." The pounding rain on the car, rolling down the windows, coupled with the lights of the road as we drove out of our estate, shadowed across Gemma's teary eyes. She held my gaze. "Do ya believe me?"

Gemma may have been our neighbour. Even come over to our house for a few drinks at Christmas, talked drunkenly about her so-so career, and how she struggled, even at her age, to make a living as a journalist. But she seemed genuine to me when we all talked and got a little pissed. But did I really believe her? At that moment did I really believe her? She was a journalist. Stuck a fuckin camera in our faces. But at that point, we didn't really have a choice. I nodded in answer to her question.

"So Mark, you will have the first TV interview after the tabs get their chance."

Roach looked over his shoulder from the driver's seat. Now we were on the country roads outside our estate, so less light. I couldn't see Roach's face. "This better not be complete shite or I bloody swear, there'll be hell to pay."

A fuckin threat?

A chorus of meows. I knew the tone: "There better be some food at this place we're goin, cos we're feckin hungry. Or there will be hell to pay."

"The kitties better be looked after. We're not worried about ourselves. We just don't want to frighten these guys." Bridget heard the tone in my voice and put a hand on my arm for the briefest second, telling me to take it easy.

The rest of the way into town we remained silent except for the intermittent cries from under the coats. And Roach's sneezing. The fucker had allergies. Twat.

I scratched Snooze under his chin and he leaned in. As he did, it hit me. Except for my jeans, I was mostly naked under the coat. We were both mostly naked under our coats.

Exposed.

Chapter

Two shifty looking journalists from *The Sun* and *The Mirror* were already in the hotel room. The room looked quite nice actually. Paid for by the papers no doubt. Two photographers, from both newspapers, hung out. They couldn't take their eyes off us and started shooting as soon as we walked in. Bridget pulled a protective arm around Leo and Molly as both cats wanted a taste of the excitement. Gemma told them she had approval of all photos used and when the photographers could shoot. The reporters gave their names to Gemma and handed over a couple of envelopes which I assumed contained the cash Gemma had negotiated. I didn't catch their names. The whirlwind of activity choked up my head, but I went with the energy. Gemma nodded to the photographers. Sitting on the edge of the bed, the camera clicks and flashes mesmerized me. Each journalist had time to pull their story, and get the legitimate proof we actually exist.

"So," *The Sun* fella asked, "does all that," and he pointed at Bridget and me and our cats, "hurt or feel weird?"

Me: "Yeah, it feels weird. But it doesn't hurt after the birth."

The fella from *The Sun* cocked a bushy eyebrow, "Birth?"

"Yeah," Bridget said. "Where do ya think they came from?"

The journalist wrote the answers down and recorded them on his mobile.

"When did it happen?"

"Snooze and Finnegan appeared two days ago," I said.

"Snooze and Finnegan?"

"That's their names."

"They have names?"

"Yes they have fuckin names."

"Ya know one of them is missing an eye?"

They were tabloid reporters, so not the brightest.

"How did he lose the eye?"

"In a poker game," I said. Bridget elbowed me. "He came like that. We don't know."

"Ya weren't walking past a place after a radiation leak, were ya?" one of them asked. "That radiation shite can cause serious mutations."

"That's a real stupid question," I flung back. But wondered about that myself for a minute.

Snooze hid down in the coat and I kept patting his head to reassure the poor fella. Finnegan showed more curiosity. Head out, he sniffed the air, gathering information, but halfway through the interviews he cried out for food, which set off Molly and Leo. Gemma asked Roach to run out to the local Spar market and get some tins of chicken dinner and some tuna. We sent him back a second time cos Molly wouldn't eat the chicken and preferred beef and gravy. And still the questions persisted. And still the interviewers and photographers wanted to touch our titty kitties. We let the two journalists touch our cats, but all they received were hisses. Bridget glanced nervously at me, cos she wasn't used to fellas wanting to touch her titties.

"They're hungry," I said, when the journalists pulled their hands away.

When Roach got back the second time with the food, I asked him to open the new tins for Molly, just to be an annoying bollix. His scowl said it all. After, he stood in the corner like a cunt and watched us, waiting for his chance to get his exclusive interview, glancing at his watch in irritation. He kept sneezing.

We'd been supplied with some egg sangers, cheese and onion crisps, and some much needed water and caffeine.

"Like is it kinda kinky, ya know, having pussies growing from yer boobs like that? Has it helped yer love life?" *The Mirror* fella—who looked like a fatter Gérard Depardieu, if that's possible—asked, face all serious.

"What sorta question is that?" Bridget said.

Me: "Get the fuck outta here with that shite."

Bridget looked in my direction and our eyes met on common ground.

Gemma answered the door when someone knocked and a hotel person handed in a bunch of clothes. "Got ya something to wear until we can collect some stuff from your place."

The interview stopped while Bridget went into the bathroom to change. She emerged in a nice blue dress, which fitted her shape. I noticed she wasn't really overweight, more curvy. She left the top of the dress unbuttoned a little for Leo and Molly's heads. Me, I put on a nice beige shirt Bridget picked for me, and left it open so the boys hung out, milking the attention now. As the interviews progressed, our kitties calmed somewhat. They understood there was no immediate danger.

All four ate from the tins we held — they even shared, and weren't actin like animals — and purred lightly when they'd finished. Finnegan licked himself and rubbed a saliva painted white paw over his ears and head. Snooze watched, jealous no doubt of Finnegan's paws. The reporters, like twats, kept digging for any sensational aspects of our lives. Bloody eejits. We were just a boring couple. No skeletons in the closet. Nothing sensational to see here. Except we had these kitties growing out of our tits. I suppose that counts. Finally, they gave up and the interviews ended. In the background, Gemma kept giving us the thumbs up in between furiously typing away on her mobile.

After the journalists left to go write their articles and print their pictures, Gemma ordered more food. A young woman appeared at the door and came in—along with a young fella—and applied makeup to Roach's face and ours, while the young fella set up some lights.

Bridget and I sat apart on the bed, only coming together when the cats wanted to sniff each other or groom each other. Our pairs extended heads and licked each other. Again, our eyes met and I felt a sadness, which I could and couldn't explain. Does that make sense?

Gemma came over as the lighting guy staged two cameras on tripods. One behind us facing Roach and one facing us over Roach's shoulder. We sat on the edge of the bed. Gemma smiled. "So are ya ready?"

Bridget looked tired. "I feel like my head's gonna fall off with all the bleedin questions."

"You're all doing great. Seriously. This is gonna be exactly the same as all the other interviews. Except live."

My stomach turned. Beside me, Bridget's body froze. I could feel her tension jump the space between us.

"Wha?" I said. Really fucking hoping I'd heard her wrong.

"Live?" Bridget flashed me a look which asked: *Did you know anything about this?* "What does that mean?" She turned back to Gemma. Me, I just thought again of everyone who knows us, watching. I thought of the mobiles we'd both left at home and how our friends and family must be bombarding us with questions and calls. "The broadcast's going out live. The interview is being picked up by other news outlets, who're 'paying,' yes, paying for the rights to put this interview out on their channels. We're making a bucket load of money for the live interview. Who said there was no money in the feckin country. It's there when ya squeeze the right person. And the Yanks don't need squeezing. They're paying a small fortune. I have an account set up for us. . ."

The lights suddenly came on in a burst. For some reason, the lights made this real. Live real. I stood up and shoved the makeup girl outta the way. I know, I was rude, but I did apologize later. "We didn't know this was goin out bloody live. Everythin is happenin way too fast. At least if we recorded it, you fellas could edit the bits that were shite." I could feel my heart race. Finnegan and Snooze reacted to the anxiety, meowling and hissing. I wasn't thinking about myself at that moment. Bridget and our titty kitties needed protection.

The look on Roach's face, like someone just rammed a poker up his arse. "Ya signed the papers, didn't ya? This is all legal. Ya can't back out or I'll sue your ass. This is my feckin interview."

We had signed some contract. Hadn't really taken in the finer print. Gemma assured us everything looked cool.

Gemma stepped into the middle of the room. "Now, everybody calm down." She turned back to us. "I said I'll look out for you. And I will. Not tellin you the interview would be live was my bad. You did great with all those eejits from the tabloids, you'll do great here. Just another eejit."

"Hey!" Roach snapped.

Gemma ignored the personality. "Mark's goin to give you the questions beforehand to look over so there'll be no surprises. Right Mark?"

"I wasn't going to. . ."

"But ya are now." The firmness in Gemma's reply even tightened my arse muscles. Bridget tapped me on the shoulder. A little of me cracked when I saw the worry on her face. When I put my hand on hers, she nodded and I let my hand drop. She glanced down her top and nodded in. Leo and Molly popped their heads out and watched Gemma and Roach bark at each other. Finnegan, with his one free paw, pulled aside my shirt to give him and Snooze a better view.

"As their manager, I would have no hesitation in walking away from this interview right now if my clients are not comfortable." Despite being more than a foot smaller than Roach, Gemma's voice stood a foot taller. "We may have bumped uglies once," she continued. Interesting fecking addition to the narrative. "But I'm under no feckin obligation to have you be the first person to interview my friends here. Right now the clock is tickin. The tabs are filing stories. We can walk out of this room and leave you sittin here with yer cameras and yer much needed makeup. Or this interview is conducted on our terms. . ." 'Our terms' I like that. Fair play to ya, G. ". . . so you can scoop every other fucker on TV. Remember, Gay was the first to interview the Beatles on the tele. Look at his career."

If you mentioned Gay Byrne to any Irish TV personality, you brought God into the conversation.

"We have a contract. You can't just walk away because we have a contract." Roach's nose ran, his eyes were watered, and he sneezed every other bloody second.

"The amount of money we're gonna make from this. . ." Gemma stared up at him and stared him down simultaneously. "You can sue the fuck outta us and we could take it. I just got a request from a major Hollywood studio for the rights to their story."

"Hollywood?" Another look between me and Bridget.

Gemma never took her eyes off Roach, the shit-eating grin spread wide. "Yup. I'll show ya the emails. Nothing settled on yet. But I can assure you, we'll get a well negotiated price."

Roach's face fumed. "Christ! Let's just do this, okay."

Gemma turned to us. "Okay, let's do this."

Chapter

Bridget and I sat on a pink loveseat supplied with the room. Silently, we allowed the makeup person to powder us and pad us and do whatever the fuck they do. Betty the makeup girl, a dyed blond Northsider with too much makeup filling gaps and wrinkles, did a final touch up. She couldn't take her eyes off our little furry family.

"Go on," I said. "Touch 'em."

"Ah Jaysus, I don't know, now."

"Ya might as well," Bridget said.

"They're real, aren't they." She put a hand tentatively over Finnegan and Snooze's head. "Fuck, I can feel their purrs against my hand. That's deadly that is." She touched a palm to each head. The boys pushed up against her hand, marking her with their cheeks. She giggled. "That's fuckin amazin."

"Let's get this going," Roach roared.

Betty smiled. "It's a miracle, isn't it? Right?"

"I hope so," is all I could think to say back.

•

Roach turned on that painted smile he's known for on his Saturday night talk show. Lights blinded us. The cameraman gave a countdown on his fingers, 3, 2, 1. Thumbs up. A red light popped on the camera.

In our chests cats purred, but their eyes squinted against the harsh lights. Bridget and I shaded their eyes as best we could.

And Roach started. "Welcome ladies and gentlemen to *The Roach House*, with me, your host, Mark Roach. Tonight we have a special show."

Blah, blah, blah. Boring introduction. Blah, blah, blah. "And I'm the first to get an exclusive live interview with the couple. Like Gay Byrne with the Beatles. Remember that? I certainly don't. I wasn't even born." Jaysus, what a twat. I used to like this fella. "Now ladies and gentlemen, what you are about to see—though many of you have seen the raw, blurry footage sprawled across social media—is not a special effect. These are not prosthetics. We have as of this moment no medical explanation for this freak phenomenon." Fuckin freaks? Fuckin arsehole. I wanted to smack the bastard across his gob. "But they are, I personally can attest, real. Hello kitties." Roach proceeded to reach over and attempted to pet Leo and Molly, a big shit-eating grin on his face. He sneezed quickly twice and a stream of snot shot from his nose. He screamed, "Fuck!" on live telly, but continued his movement toward Leo and Molly. Both Leo and Molly hissed, their tongues vibrating in their mouths. Leo's head snapped forward and bit down on Roach's outstretched hand. I could see the needle pointed teeth plunge into his skin. Roach screamed so high you'd'a thought he'd gotten his bollix caught in a mangle. The scream set off the other three.

That's when it happened. Leo pulled back. And said, "Badddss No likesss."

Time froze. I know, a fuckin cliché. 'Holy Jaysus,' I thought.

A chorus went up. Finnegan, Snooze, Leo, and Molly screamed, hissed, "Badddsss." Hisses.

Yeah. Crazy, right? Our titty kitties cats could talk.

Chapter

Roach stumbled backward. Another sneeze burst from his nose. Betty the makeup girl, while initially shocked, bust out laughing when Roach fell back onto his chair—which proceeded to tip backward—a snot shower splattering his face like a money shot.

Finnegan started yelling, "Fightsss, we fightsss." Deep in my body, the close connection with Snooze and Finnegan compelled me to follow their emotional state.

Snooze screamed, "Runsss, we runnnsss."

Concerned, Gemma shot toward us. "What's happening? I didn't know they could talk."

I pushed past her, Bridget behind me. "Neither did we."

Gemma grabbed me by the arm. "Where ya goin?"

"We're gettin outta here," I said.

I reached back for Bridget, and she took my hand.

Roach flailed around on the floor screaming, blood pumping from the bite on his hand. At the same time he tried to wipe the snot from his face. "My face. My fuckin hand." His Dublin accent came thick and chunky. His RTE smooth personality evaporated live in front of the whole country. The world. "I'll fuckin sue the arses off ya. I fuckin swear." The cameraman attempted to quiet the presenter, reminding him they were still recording. "I don't give a bollix. Look at me bleedin hand. It's bleedin. Get me somethin to stop the bleedin bleedin."

As Bridget passed Roach she flipped him off. "Arsehole."

Leo and Molly hissed, "Arsssseholesss." Bridget's titty kitty nipple cats were also now verbal, it appeared, with mouths on them like their mother.

"Where ya gonna go?" Gemma pulled on her coat, her mobile up, recording every moment.

"Don't know, but we can't stay here," I said. "It's gettin fuckin ridiculous."

As soon as I pulled the door open, we heard voices in the hall, harsh and commanding. I popped my head out—Finnegan and Snooze craned their necks.

"We runsss?" Snooze's excitement rumbled from my chest and I could feel his and Finnegan's fight or flight instincts leap and bounce through my system. I could also feel Bridget's energy pulsing through her strong hand and up my arm, which seemed to send sparks through my tits and kitties, completing a circuit.

"They're in this room," a male voice cried.

Two An Garda Síochána exited the lift at the end of the hall and started in our direction. A spotty fucker in a suit and tie pointed at us. "That's them." One of the hotel staff. Must've spread the word.

"How'ya folks," the taller Garda said, his Cork accent real obvious. "I'm gonna have to ask ya to stop there, now."

Despite the fact we'd done nothing wrong, my first inclination was to run. The Gardai must've seen this in our body language.

"Ah, now, there's no need for that," the smaller Garda said. His accent thick Dublin, not unlike mine. But he looked Chinese. The new Ireland.

"Runss, fightsss, we runsss, we fightssss," said Finnegan. Cats love contradictions. You just never know what's going on in those furry little heads of theirs. They want pets, they want to scratch. They want to cuddle, they want to bite. Finnegan wanted both to fight and run.

We decided to pick one option. To cat cries of protest and fear, our family ran.

Chapter

Down the backstairs.

"This is mad," Bridget said as we bounced our way down the steps.

Gemma held her mobile.

"What the hell are ya doin?" I said.

"Streaming live."

"Stop, stop," Finnegan and Snooze were yelling as their heads flipped and flopped.

Leo yelled "Jaysussss," and sounded more Dublin than me.

Molly's exclamation sounded a little more urgent. "Pee. Pee."

"Shite," Bridget said. "We really need to take a wee."

I shot her a look. "Are ya fuckin serious?"

"Yeah, we're fuckin serious. Last time I peed was back at the house."

We hit the last step on the last floor. To our right I saw an EXIT.

"This is like one of those found footage movies," Gemma said. "Except, live."

I ignored her and pulled Bridget toward the exit. I slammed on the bar and we broke out into the pouring rain. And the flashing lights.

Blue flashing lights strobed across our eyes and the surrounding walls of the hotel. Bridget and I immediately covered our kitties, protecting their sensitive little eyes. Beyond the lights I could see shapes moving, coming closer.

I saw the military outfits first. A large bearded fella walked toward us, his hands up in a show of peace. "It's okay, folks. We're not here to hurt ya. We just need to talk, is all."

I'd describe the accent as educated. Don't know why I'd say that, but he sounded like a Trinity student or something.

Bridget squeezed my hand tight and I squeezed back. The feckin military. Like something out of an alien invasion movie or ET. Shite like this never happens in Ireland.

Finnegan pushed my hand out of his eyes and squinted. "Mess seess. I bravessss. Mess seesss."

"Okay, buddy, you can see." I took away my hand.

Snooze trembled. "We go awaysss again. We go awaysss." His voice cracked, fragile, thin as a After Eight mint chocolate.

I kissed him on the head. "Stay calm, buddy."

Bridget watched me and kissed the top of Leo and Molly's heads.

The military fella stepped closer. "Jaysus! They do talk."

Gemma held her mobile up, recording. "This is goin live, so you can't harm us."

"We're not gonna harm ya. Look, my name is General Mike Ross. And I'm just here to protect you and your. . ."

"Titty kitties." I finished.

"Nipple cats," Bridget said.

"Okay. Your titty kitties," Ross said and I felt I'd just won a strategic military victory. "Jaysus, I can't believe they're real."

"They're real," Bridget growled. "And they're scared."

Except Finnegan. He hissed and struck out with his paws, but they just wheeled in the air.

"Look," Ross went on. "My job is to get you to a safe place so some people can talk to you. That's it. Some doctors and some higher ups want to talk about what's happening here. Everyone believed all this. . ." he pointed ". . .was a joke, ya know? But the more we watched you guys. . . The more. . . The more fascinated everyone became. What you have there, are. . . weird—"

"They're bloody cats." I shouted.

Finnegan hissed out, "We kittiesss. Ssssscratch. Sssave perssson Meeky and perssson Breegitss." Well, there ya go. Our cats knew our names. Well, at least at that moment I knew Finnegan knew our names.

Ross stepped closer. Behind him men in uniform shifted. "We're not here to do anything to hurt you. As I said. What's happening here, to say the least, is bloody strange. Right? We have some people who want to help. My orders are to bring you in for a wee chat."

"Buggerss awaysss." The sound came from Bridget's chest. Molly's damp, furry head popped up.

"Leo!" Bridget shot back, "Take it easy." Leo croaked out a voice, husky and deep, like he lived in a cave. When Leo's courage kicked in, he'd be the first, when people came around, to spring from where he'd hidden, the first to attack legs and toes, particularly when protecting his sister. Now, once again. . . Molly's head disappeared below again, probably shaking and shivering. The chaos a little overwhelming.

"Does that black and white cat have only one eye?"

"Yeah, he fuckin does," Bridget barked. "What is it with everyone and my one-eyed cat?"

Ross ignored her. "We have some doctors who want to make sure this isn't. . . ya know, infectious or anythin."

Bridget and I shared a puzzled look. Back to General Ross. "What's with all the soldiers and Garda?"

"Just makin sure you come with us for a little while. So you and those things will be safe."

"They're not bloody things," Bridget spat. "They've names. This is Leo and Molly," she continued, pointing down. "And that's Snooze and Finnegan." I pointed my own introductions. The General simply nodded. But like he didn't give a shite.

"How'd you know we were here?" I asked.

"Yeah," Gemma said. "I made sure to keep everything on the QT."

"I'm told one of the reporters. . ."

"Bloody reporters!" Gemma shot back. "Least we got their money."

The General took a step forward. "Let's get out of the rain. We can talk on the way."

"Where?" Bridget asked. "Where are we goin?"

"Not far."

"How far is not far?" I asked.

"We fightsss now, okay, okay." Finnegan said, his courage rock solid to my core. Snooze trembled below. Afraid we might lose each other again. "Yes, yes, runss bloody runss." Finnegan pawed the air, his claws out and scraping.

Ross couldn't take his eyes from my boys as they yelled. "I gave you my word you'll be safe," Ross said.

The reality? We had nowhere left to bloody go. Behind Ross came more movement.

Gemma, Bridget and I huddled. "What do ya wanna do?" I asked.

"We fighttsss," Finnegan replied. "Meeky and Breegit personss fightsss."

"We runss. All we runss," Snooze cried low. "Ssstay togetherss. Never leave."

I kissed the top of their heads. "That's right. We're sticking together."

Bridget kissed Molly and Leo.

Ross stared at us. "Those cats are really fucking talking, aren't they?"

"Yes, for the last time they're really fuckin talkin," Gemma snapped.

"We have to go with them, don't we?" Bridget sounded defeated.

"Where else we gonna go?" I said.

We were still holding hands.

Chapter

The journey lacked excitement, mainly because we weren't transported in a military vehicle under military guard. That would've been kinda cool. General Ross drove us in a Humvee, while the minions of the army followed behind, their powerful lights washed out the inside of the Humvee. Bridget and me in the back, Gemma in the front, her mobile in Ross' face.

"Can ya get that outta my face?" Ross boomed.

"No. We're streaming live."

"You know we could shut you down, right?" the General said.

"Tell that to the millions watching live," Gemma shot back. Ross said nothing.

As we drove through the pelting rain, the squeak of the windscreen wipers sounded like cats screaming for dinner. Which once again set our titty kitties on a piercing chorus.

"Meat musssh," Molly cried. "We wantss meat musssh."

They sounded like little kids.

"Meatsss mush," Leo said and batted Molly on the head. She tried to swat his paw.

"We're gonna have to get these guys some food pretty soon," Bridget said. "They don't behave the best when they're hungry. Plus, we need to hit the bathroom."

"Yeah." I shifted in the backseat. "I could really go for a good shite."

Though it may have been Snooze or Finnegan wanted going.

"When we get to the base, we'll let you all go to a bathroom," said Ross.

No way I'd tell these fuckers about our shared systems. Finnegan somehow let me know I needed the shite. He and his brother were just fine.

"So, General Ross," asked Gemma. "Do you know what will happen to me and my friends? Remember, we're live."

"Look, Ma'am," Ross started.

"Gemma!"

"Look Gemma. This isn't a big American movie with mad special effects and car chases. Our doctors saw all this happening on tele, and like everyone, they were fascinated. We want to make sure that we've got nothing contagious or something."

"Like nipple cats can be contracted or somethin?" Bridget asked.

"Titties kitties," I reminded her.

"Is that what they're called?"

"Yes," said Bridget. "Nipple cats. As good a name as any, wha?" She turned her head and smiled at me.

Not as good as titty kitties, I thought.

Chapter

We saw very little of the exterior of our location as we were escorted from the Humvee into a large brick building.

Corridors followed. The sound of boots on the concrete floors. Meows. And purrs. Cats purr when they're either happy, or nervous. The purr can be a security blanket, a soothing rumble when a situation becomes stressful. The connection I had with Finnegan and Snooze (and I assumed the one between Bridget, Molly, and Leo), felt heightened in these moments of stress. Smells and sounds sharpened. I smelt the sweat oozing from Bridget's pores. I could smell Finnegan and Snooze's breath, raw and meaty from the food they'd eaten a few hours before. I was aware of Ross's own damp stink under his uniform. I could also smell the fact I didn't trust the uniformed fucker.

Ross stopped before a large metal door. A "hazardous waste" symbol on the outside.

"Why don't you wait in here," Ross said. The soldiers who accompanied us halted and waited behind us. Ross pressed a code into a pad on the wall and the door hissed like a last gasp and opened. On the threshold, Bridget, me, and Gemma stuck our heads in. The room looked very clinical, metal tables, worrying shite like that.

The four cats started growling. Like really growling. Dog-like growls. My awareness sharpened and my body tensed. Bridget appeared to have the same awareness, because she flashed a look at me, and I could see fear in her eyes. But what could we do? Fight the whole feckin Irish army?

I stepped in first and Bridget immediately mirrored me. Gemma just crossed through when Ross said, "We would like to talk to you, separately."

Gemma lowered the camera, looked at us. A spike of fear in her eyes. I grabbed Gemma by the hand and pulled her into the room with us. "She bloody stays with us," I stood in front of the journalist. Gemma seemed to come to her senses and started using her mobile again.

Ross looked unfazed, as if he expected the reaction. He nodded, like he'd just done us a feckin favour. He stepped out and the door closed. A hiss of breath came again. We were sealed in.

Chapter

"Leo, Molly, peepeesss," Molly said in a low purring cadence.

I walked to the door and banged. "We need to use the bog. Hello?"

Bridget approached the door. Banged. "I swear, we're gonna just go in the feckin sink over there. Leo and Molly need to use the bathroom. We need to use the bathroom." She looked up to the corner of the ceiling and noticed the camera. "We know you can see us."

"She's not jokin," I said. "She'll piss in yer sink."

"Aw fuck!" Bridget looked down. A wet dribble scurried down her leg. "Too fuckin late." Bridget hugged Leo and Molly, forgiving the two for not being able to hold on any longer. "It's alright, guys."

"We weess," Molly meowed.

"We weess," Leo echoed.

"I know ya weed," she said softly. "I know."

Gemma turned her camera on the camera in the corner and yelled. "The world can see what you're doing."

"Shite." Bridget turned scarlet. "Ya didn't just film us takin a piss did ya?"

"No. Yer good. Just the puddle," Gemma replied.

"Wha the fuck!" Bridget rushed toward Gemma. "Ya can't just show the whole world us takin a piss. That's private."

"Are ya sure?" I said.

"Sure what?" Bridget asked.

"Sure the whole world is watchin us."

"The mobile's on." Gemma pointed. Steaming live.

Finnegan rested a paw on Snooze, to comfort his cat buddy.

"Ya think the military were gonna let us just film what they're doin?" A dribble slid down my inner thigh. "Crap! One of the boys just took a piss." Now we were both standing in piss.

Chapter

Bridget sat on the floor, her back against the wall, her chin tilted to her chest. She wasn't asleep. I heard her comfort Molly and Leo. She marked them with her face, and they marked her back. We'd been there close to two hours with not a word or bleedin action. I circled the room like a fuckin moron trying to calm Finnegan who just wanted to fight. Not sure who he wanted to fight. There were only seven of us in the room. He repeated "We fightss. We bitess." Over and over.

Until, "Bitesss," Leo started to join in. I sat down beside my wife.

Gemma continued to film the interior of the room, a running commentary came angry and barbed. She switched to her mobile service and dialed. After a few seconds she disconnected and said, "Still no fuckin signal." She chose another wall and sat down, knees up like me and Bridget. "I'm really tired, ya know?" We did. "I just wanted to be a journalist. My da was an electrician from Tallaght. Me mam was a housewife and could hardly read." Her accent moved from an RTE radio neutral into something betraying her Dublin roots. "Thought movin to the suburbs would be a step up. But now I live in a ghost town. Know what I mean?" We did. "Jaysus, I can't even find a fella. I work all the bleedin time, there's no more time left in the day. Know what I mean?" We did. "The mortgage is up to here." She demonstrated with her hands the level of her mortgage. "We have all this money in the account I set up, by the way." I liked the sound of that. "But if we're not gonna make it outta here, what the fuck's the point?" My thoughts rummaged around the same lines. "Me da would be laughin his arse off at me right now for givin up the job workin as secretary in his electrician business."

"Well, this is more exciting, isn't it?" I said.

She lifted her eyes and shot a look. She gave no more exposition after the look.

Finnegan and Snooze sniffed the air around Molly and Leo. And communicated. I could hear the mumbles in my head. My brain attempting to translate. But the sounds were just echoes right now, like they were coming from underwater. We were all connected now.

The pee I'd let loose in me pants had turned cold. Really uncomfortable.

Bridget's body felt close. "How ya doin?" I looked at my wife and pushed a weak smile onto my lips.

Bridget shook her head. A shake of recognition for a hopeless situation. Our relationship.

I reached along the ground and found her hand. Her fingers tightened around my hand, and the grip felt warm, and I fuckin swear I felt her blood pumping through her veins.

"Isn't this some crazy fucked up shite we have goin on here?" she said.

"That's one way to put it." My fingers weren't going to let loose from hers. I needed them. I didn't want to slip from the cliff, so I held on.

A pause, then, "Ya know what?"

She left the question at the edge of the cliff, looking down at me.

"What?"

"I'm glad we're goin through this together, ya know?" I did. "I'm glad I'm on this adventure, with you, with Leo and Molly. And with Snooze and Finnegan."

Finnegan heard his name. His head turned to me. Inside my head, I heard him say, "We fightsss." He started to shift inside me, and used his front paws to pull and wriggle. His body jerked, struggled, and twisted, stretching my skin. I sat watching. And let it happen. I took the pain as it happened. Finnegan pulled and pulled away from my tits, until he let out a yowl of triumph, and dropped to the floor between my legs, fully formed. Newborn. The hole in my tit he'd just fallen through closed behind him, like a flap. It didn't quite seal or heal over. "Wess fightsss. Meeky."

Gemma dumbstruck.

Bridget wide eyed.

Despite having felt it. Witnessed it. I was still, "What the fuck!?"

Chapter

All three of us. . . sorry, all seven of us, watched Finnegan find his feet. My big, brave white furred boy brushed against my legs, marking me as his own. His claws grabbed for my thighs and he sharpened his nails like I was his personal tree trunk.

After the initial 'What the fuck,' I accepted this new development. I have to admit, nothing really surprised me anymore. The last few days had thrown us some weird, fucked up shite. This kinda fucked up and weird didn't really feel as fucked up and weird as it probably should've. My main questions in the moment were, where did he keep his hind legs when inside me? And why wasn't there any blood, or goo coming from my body? Our bodies. Nothing leaked from the exit Finnegan had come from, and there was still no pain.

"We fightss, yesss?" Finnegan continued sharpening his nails on my knees, stretching his body, like he loved the new space he'd been rewarded.

Snooze, Molly, and Leo cocked their heads at each other. I heard Snooze's voice. "Me wantss awayss! Helpsss awayss!" His tone, pitched higher than Finnegan's, contained more trepidation. "Sssscaredss! But fightsss!"

Finnegan replied, "Fightsss, togethersss. Yesss. Protectsss."

That set Snooze off. My ginger tom struggled to force his way through my other tit, stretching his neck. He had a harder time than Finnegan. His paws were still inside. I lay my legs flat along the ground and Finnegan leapt onto my thighs. He reached his front paws around Snooze's head, and with claws extended, began to pull his cat friend from my body.

Gemma crouched down, two hands holding her mobile. She wasn't going to miss this event.

Bridget watched in stunned silence. As did Molly and Leo. Taking everything in. Learning.

Snooze moved back and forth as Finnegan pulled. He screamed in pain. Finnegan's claws were digging into his cheeks and neck.

"Hold up, buddy," I said. Finnegan sat back on his haunches as I untangled my fingers reluctantly from Bridget's and wrapped my hands around Snooze's orange neck, and with slow movements so as not to hurt my furry pal, I pulled. I could feel Snooze work from the inside, aiding me. When his cat shoulders appeared, I pulled from under his forelegs.

"Friendss, friendss," Finnegan chanted.

Molly and Leo started the chant. "Freess. Pullsss. Ussss. Freess. We fightsss."

Snooze came slowly. Pull. First leg. Pull. Second leg. Finnegan jumped onto my thighs again and resumed his pull, gripping Snooze's fur tightly. Snooze wailed. "Painss. Friendss. Painss."

"I know, buddy," I said. "Nearly there."

My skin stretched to accommodate Snooze's body. This birth was way more painful than Finnegan's. A few more tugs. Snooze's ginger body slipped out. No gore. A little goo. The hole in my nipple, similar to the one Finnegan emerged through, contracted, but didn't completely seal. The pain of birth dissipated after Snooze came free.

As soon as Snooze fell onto my legs, Finnegan started licking his head. Then mutual grooming. I felt a little like a voyeur to be honest. Both cats rubbed forcefully against each other like long separated brothers.

I looked up at Bridget, and for the first time since all this crazy shite began. I felt bloody joy. Tears filled her eyes and each one sparkled like a diamond. Instinctually I leaned over, pulled her close to me, and she rested her head against my chest.

Then we heard the door breathe out, the vacuum breaking, and things went to bollix.

Chapter

Three men in white coats stood in the doorway, masks over their faces. All three were easy to identify for description purposes. Like the three bears, one was tall, bald. The next smaller, slightly more hair, which he'd swept into a comb over. The last was a small fella, about 5' 4", a nice head of hair, but oily, unwashed. All three smiled under their covered faces. I knew cos their eyes crinkled at the edges where their masks couldn't cover. Fake smiles. No lightness touched their pupils.

The little fella stepped forward. "Hello, my name is Dr. Newman." Behind him by the door, I saw armed soldiers. I hadn't noticed weapons before, when we were escorted in, but they were carrying them now. Something had changed since we'd arrived. The soldiers looked nervous as they attempted to peer into the room around the lab coats. I pushed myself up from the floor. Finnegan hissed, jerked forward and back. His fur spiked like a porcupine. Snooze appeared to spit rather than hiss, but he stayed close to my legs and remained in contact like he needed the reassurance of my presence. Leo and Molly yowled. Bridget covered them protectively.

"And?" I said, replying to shortie's introduction.

He stepped closer. Hisses and spitting and yowling backed him off.

Snooze clawed his way up my leg. I winced as he dug into my crotch for better grip, then he pulled himself into my arms.

"That's amazing," Newman said. "Quite bizarre and bloody amazing." His accent not quite Irish. A hint of sharp German pushed through, like one of those movie Nazis, but had been curved over with a Dublin accent. Like the two had reluctantly fused together. "I have been watching you two with an acute fascination since you appeared to us all. I simply knew I had to have you." He quickly corrected himself. "Had to meet you, that is." He continued to stare. Unforgettable to say the least. "They've evolved. Started in the breast area and are now, free roam?" He narrowed his eyes and stared at Bridget. Mostly at Leo. "Does the black and white one only have one eye?"

Bridget and I in tandem: "Piss the fuck off!"

Newman didn't appear to care we were telling him to fuck off. "How did this happen?"

Gemma stepped up. The girl's got balls. "We want to know where we are." I could see Gemma's mobile phone battery starting to fade. "Fuck!" she said and shook the thing like she could shake it back to life.

"All in good time, madame," Newman said. "We just need to know what we have here. Yes? We want to know it's not. . . well, contagious."

Finnegan wound around my legs but kept a wary eye on everyone else in the room. Contagious? I thought. "Contagious?" I said. "What the fuck you on about? Do they look contagious? They're healthy cats." Then I realized something. "Okay, granted, they haven't been for a vet check up in a long time. . ."

"Look at what we have here," Newman said, gesturing to us, but more for the benefit of the white coats behind him. "You have an animal growing from your breast. These are biological entities and therefore may have the potential to harbor or spread disease."

"Then we have the disease, too. Cos they came from us. And there's no way you're gonna touch these guys." I pointed to Snooze, Finnegan, and Bridget's boobs. "Or us for that matter."

"Fuckin try, yis fucks." Bridget has a mouth on her when she wants.

I held an arm out protecting us all. "It'll be over our dead bodies. And before ya give me one of those movie villain smiles and say something like, 'if you insist,' just look at the mobile and say cheese."

The smile from Newman broadened. "Oh, you will be relieved of your camera."

Gemma flinched. "Over my dead body, yis fucks. This is mine. We have live streaming going out right now."

"We blocked the signal hours ago," the bald fucker behind Newman said. "Scrambled. Very easy, all we did—"

"Does not matter." Newman stepped closer. "We just wanted to make sure there were no potential parasites or aliens—"

"Fuckin aliens!" I felt the sharpness in my throat when I hocked that out. "Yer talkin aliens, now? These aren't fuckin aliens. They came out of our tits, not from outer space. All those people across the world saw us on TV. You can't dismiss that, now can ya, ya stupid gobshite?"

"Hoax." The smirk came through in his eyes. "The spin is already being spun. Like Orson Welles and *The War of the Worlds*."

The three of us shared a look, asking each other the same question: Is he lying?

Newman stepped forward again. "We have the whole world believe. . ." He pointed at three of us. ". . .you all perpetrated a huge hoax. No one will believe your stories. Special effects are wonderful these days."

"Once they see us, they'll believe," Bridget said. "This can't be faked." Bridget pointed at Molly and Leo's head with a decisive finger.

"You will not have to worry about all that." Newman's eyes crinkled again behind the mask. "Now, we will start by getting an X-ray of your bodies. Myself and my colleagues. . ." he pointed at the other bears, "Dr. Burke," with the comb over, "and Dr. Smythe," the tall fucker, "will have to look at the cats. See what constitutes their body chemistry. MRIs. And other procedures." Three soldiers moved farther into the room and stood beside the doctors. The nervous energy and fear coming from these soldiers was kinda sad. These fellas had training and guns and god knows what else, and still they were afraid of us and our titty kitties. "We'll make sure you get a good night's sleep before we start with our investigation," Newman continued. "These two. . ." He gestured to Snooze and Finnegan. ". . .seeing as they have already exited the body, we will take them and start tonight. They will be well taken care of, I assure you."

Finnegan clawed his way up my leg and I cradled him in my arm right beside Snooze. The boys seemed to understand Newman's intentions, and tightened their grip on my body, claws digging into flesh. They hurt less when they were inside me. Gemma still held up her mobile, despite the fact the bloody thing was about as effective as a piece of crusty shite. Instinct I suppose.

Bridget stepped closer and I felt the pull of her body heat. Her chest heaved. Breath heavy. Panic. Fear. And an energy a little harder to place, pulled us together. Leo and Molly hissed. Leo's mouth opened and a sound formed, rumbled through Bridget's body and jumped across to mine, and I could hear Leo's voice in my head. The first letter came out as a rolling "R" as if Leo were experimenting with the feel of language on his tongue. He followed this with a curved vibration, as he completed the word and sound, with an "un."

Our cats were riled. Instinct bloomed through us. Despite their migration from my body, I still felt very much connected to Finnegan and Snooze, and I felt their intention and fear. Fight or flight. Or a judicious combination of the two. Bridget felt the same, I could tell just by her body language. I knew she had connected with Finnegan and Snooze. She finally accepted them and they accepted her. I'm not talkin bollix here, despite how it may sound: some airy-fairy, new agey, Kenny G shite. It kinda felt like we were all one being. Not like the Borg or anything.

Newman tilted his head to us, but the gesture was intended for the guards. Two of them moved forward and jerked their weapons toward the door. Gemma and Bridget looked at me like they were waiting for me to make the next move. I didn't have a clue what to do, and we didn't have a choice.

We filed from the white room and into the bland corridor we'd come through a few hours previous. Bridget slipped her hand in mine. She kissed the tops of Leo and Molly's heads. I could hear them purring. The bad kind. The purr a cat makes when self-soothing. Their irises huge, like solid black marbles

Finnegan had climbed down from my arms and walked at my feet, his body tight with tension. He glanced over his shoulder. Behind us, soldiers diligently covered us with weapons. Still the fear in their eyes. Did we look that dangerous? Snooze lay in my arm, clinging to the material of my coat, his body held tense as an elastic band. He felt solid. All muscle.

Gemma walked just ahead of us. Her mobile may be useless live, but she held it tightly in her hand by her leg. Still no one had taken the thing away from her. The three doctors, or whatever the fuck they were, led the way to fuck knows where.

The end of the poorly lit corridor T-ed left and right. Newman snapped his fingers. One of the guards stepped forward and took Bridget by the arm and pulled her back in the direction we'd just come. Leo and Molly hissed wildly, swiftly swiping, their claws extended, attempting to scratch the soldier dragging them. But he stayed just out of reach of their claws.

Bridget struggled to break from the guard's hold. She planted herself to the spot. The young soldier wasn't gonna move her if she didn't want to move. The poor fella didn't expect the sudden stop and lost his grip, staggered back.

"What the fuck!" Bridget screamed.

I echoed her surprise. Instantly another soldier turned a weapon on me. Finnegan, on the ground, arched his back, and spat up at the soldier. The soldier's muzzle swung down to Finnegan. Newman and I screamed in tandem, "No!"

The soldier drew back.

"What's goin on?" I screamed, my voice high. Gemma pressed herself against the wall of the corridor, frightened, but also refusing to move. "Where are they goin?"

Finnegan raced up my leg and disappeared with Snooze into my coat. Pain shot through me as I felt them clamber back inside me. My flesh closed behind them like a seam. The soldier paled, and looked to Newman for an explanation and instructions. He didn't get any. But Newman looked fascinated by this development.

"Amazing," Newman kinda whispered to himself.

Dr Smythe, the tall arsehole, moved toward Bridget and the soldier. Again, the soldier yanked on her arm. Bridget wasn't having any of that shite. She used her weight like an anchor.

"They'll be fine," Newman said. His smooth voice still held some Nazi, so I didn't believe a feckin word comin outta that gob of his. "We'll just be asking her a few questions before we start our studies."

I locked eyes with Bridget. Our years together suspended between us in the gaze. She wanted to trust me. I could see her need to trust me. In that moment, Daniel Day Lewis's voice popped into my head and I screamed at her, "I will find you. No matter how long it takes, or how far. I will find you." Bridget looked confused. As did everyone else. It took a moment to click. She shook her head, a 'ya sad bollix' smile lit her face. I'd just used a line from *Last of the Mohicans*. She knew I hated Daniel Day fuckin Lewis. Despite the poxy lighting, I could see crystal tears flicker from her eyes.

"Ya feckin better," she said, then proceeded to stamp a foot on the soldier's instep. He screamed in pain, but recovered quickly, and dragged her away, Smythe trailing awkwardly behind, like a giraffe with hemorrhoids.

"You better not hurt her or our cats, or I swear I'll shove one of those guns up your fuckin arse. . ."

"My colleague won't harm her," Newman replied. Gestured with his head and another armed soldier grabbed Gemma and pulled her from the wall. She slipped her mobile into her pocket, which no one seemed to notice.

"You touch me and I swear I'll bring the *Irish Independent* down on your head." The soldier held her, but threw a worried look to Newman. Newman shook his head as if assuring the soldier. Then they disappeared at the T to the right. "Hey fuckface. . ." was all I heard as she too disappeared.

Somewhere in the facility, I could still hear Bridget yelling obscenities. That made me happy. Until I was alone in the corridor with Newman and Burke, his comb over needing some over, and the last armed guard.

"Where are we goin?" I asked.

"To further science and explore new worlds," Newman said like a pretentious twat.

Inside me, Snooze and Finnegan shifted. Alert. Inside my head, Finnegan's voice burned. "Weeess fightsss." My cats' voices were changing, becoming more distinct, acquiring personalities.

Weeess Fightsss. Ya better fuckin believe it.

Chapter

The room looked similar to the one we'd just been held in. More medical equipment. I hadn't a clue what they did, but I recognized them from movies. Machines that go *ping*.

Newman and Burke stood in the doorway. The soldier, rigid and smelling of fear—I was smelling what my boys were smelling—blocked the exit.

Newman stepped into the room. "Dr. Burke," Newman said, his back to his colleague, "can you see to the other subjects. . . Bridget?" I turned to face them. Newman tilted his head. "Her name is Bridget, yes?"

I took a step toward him. "Yeah."

The guard swung his weapon directly at me. Newman gestured the weapon down. The guard obeyed. "We won't need any of that, will we?"

"What's gonna happen to Bridget and Gemma?"

"Absolutely nothing harmful I assure you," Newman stepped closer. "Dr. Burke, please see to it that you and Dr. Smythe treat this man's wife and breast pets with respect."

Breast pets? Not bad, but nowhere near as catchy as titty kitties. Am I right?

Newman made no eye contact with Burke but kept that arsehole of a smile through the mask.

"Yes sir." Burke left the room and closed the door behind him. Nothing now but the awkward silence and smell of antiseptic. Newman waved a hand toward an examination table. "We're going to take some X-rays and see where we'll go from there. Now that doesn't sound too bad, does it?" Condescending wanker. "You've been X-rayed before, yes?"

"For a broken toe at Mount Carmel Hospital. Not on a military base to check out my tits to make sure my cats aren't feckin aliens." I was quite chuffed with my sarcasm.

"Not many people have," Newman replied, a smug smile again creasing the white mask. He suddenly seemed to realize he wore a mask. He pulled it over his head and threw it to the floor. "I don't think you're contagious, do you?"

"I hope I am, you pretentious turd gutter. I hope y'all get nipple cats." I shot a look at the soldier. He took a step back like I'd put a feckin curse on his family. "And why didn't they give you fellas masks?"

The soldier seemed to ponder that for a second.

Newman stood stone faced. Without the mask he really looked like a Nazi. I could've just been projecting, but I'd seen pictures of Nazis before, and Newman definitely had the Nazi vibe.

Newman moved to an examination table in the corner of the room. "Now if you could take off your coat and lay back on the table."

"Fuck no."

Newman once again used some type of silent communication with the soldier. The gun came up.

"You gonna kill me? I don't fuckin think so."

"Even with you dead, we could still get an X-ray." His eyes didn't lie. "I'd rather not have to do anything drastic. But I will."

I moved slowly to the table. "So much for not wantin to hurt us,"

"I am a man of science, but. . ."

"Science comes first?"

He shrugged.

"What about all those questions you were gonna ask before the studies?"

"I don't need questions. I will have all the answers I need as soon as we start the experiments. . . Sorry, I meant examination."

"Twat!" I said. I began to slip off the coat. Finnegan and Snooze shifted inside me. Agitated and grumbling. I could feel their sharp claws pulling at my skin. I held back a wince. I hoped they wouldn't make a habit of making biscuits on my insides in the future.

Would Newman actually follow through with his threat or was the fucker just bluffing? His eyes weren't. But plenty of arseholes can posture with their eyes.

I took time with my striptease. "What if you killed me and these two died too? You wouldn't have anythin."

"Well that's a good point. I would have my soldier friend here shoot you in the kneecap. If that didn't work, then the other kneecap. And so on. So I could keep you alive but in pain. How does that sound?"

Good point. The coat came off and slipped to the floor. I looked down at my tits. Finnegan and Snooze were nowhere in sight. They had completely sealed themselves inside, a slight scar like a mouth, the only evidence of the exit and entrance to their titty cat house.

"Where are they?" Newman asked.

"They've gone into hibernation."

"Don't get stupid with me," Newman said. "Get them out."

"They've gone back to their home planet. How about that?" As I said it, that shite sounded as plausible as anything else. "They'll only come out when they're ready."

The soldier aimed the weapon at my knee.

•

I moved quickly to the table. Laid back. My stomach sat in my eyeline like a hillock with course black scrub. Goosebumps popped up on my skin from the cold and not a little fear. The paper spread on the exam table took in some of the cold. I felt like I needed to take a dump. That pressure down below sent burbles through my insides. Could also be coming from the boys. Finnegan and Snooze reacted to the gassy rumbles and shifted inside me. In my head I told them to stay put. For now. "Here ya go," I said. "Take yer bloody X-ray. They're in there and not comin out. So go fuck yerself." Mad images shot through my head: Newman cutting me open and pulling Finnegan and Snooze from my tits like screaming newborns all covered in a sticky mess. The boys shifted with anxiety, like they could see the violent images and started to freak out.

Newman didn't give a shite. "They'll either come out when they're hungry, or with enough. . . shall we say. . . sensory encouragement. But the X-ray will do for now." Newman told the young fella in the uniform to lower the weapon. He stared down at me. "You are fascinating."

"Thanks very much."

"I have seen many things in my life as a scientist, but few unearthly events like this."

I wondered what other crazy shite he'd seen and started to imagine different animals popping out of various orifices. Then I pictured Finnegan and Snooze as half cyborg, machine guns attached to their paws, rising over hills, going into battle. Mad it was.

"What are you fellas gonna do?" I asked. "Weaponize my titty kitties?"

I heard Bridget yelling in me head, "They're nipple cats."

Newman didn't crack a smile, like what I'd just said wasn't idiotic, and that maybe weaponizing our titty kitties wasn't as stupid idea as it sounded. How'd they'd do that, I hadn't a clue. Seriously, how in the fuck could you weaponize titty kitties? Or nipple cats. Whatever.

Newman turned his back to me. Fiddled around on some table. Metal clanked and there were the general sounds one doesn't want to hear in a hospital. The guard's eyes flicked for a second to the doc, then quickly flicked back to watching me.

Newman turned and I saw the syringe in his hand. I jerked up from the table. "What the fuck ya doin with that?"

"It's just a sedative."

"To take a feckin an X-ray? I don't think so."

Newman shot a wordless order to the guard and the big fuck glided over in a blink.

Newman held the needle up in one hand and gestured with his other. "Give me your arm."

I didn't.

"Give me your arm, please. I promise, you'll only feel a small prick."

"Yeah, well you're a fuckin big prick." Not a smile. The bastard. No sense of humour.

"If you don't give me your arm, your lack of cooperation will reflect badly on not only you, but your wife. And your pets."

"You touch my wife's titties and I'll bate the shite outta ya."

"I am not interested in your wife's 'titties.' Her pussies, yes." He did crack a smile, but now I'd lost my sense of humour.

I extended my arm. On my inner elbow crease, I saw a big blue vein waiting to be violated. I've always had prominent veins. This big blue treacherous bastard sat up on my skin waiting for his moment.

The needle slipped easily into my skin. I could feel the cold liquid seep into my bloodstream and imagined a cloud like a cauliflower push the blood away as it entered the channel. I must've gone under pretty quick. Light sedative my arse. Before I slipped away, I could feel Finnegan and Snooze, their hearts racing, but their purrs silent.

Stay where you are boys. Stay where you are.

Chapter

When my eyes finally opened, they felt gritty, like someone had rubbed sand on my eyeballs while I slept. As my mind became more focused, I checked to see if Finnegan and Snooze were with me, but I couldn't feel anything under my skin. No movement. No sound. No purr. I could feel them in my head but couldn't see them. I panicked. Tears came and I felt a strong emotional purge pour from my eyes. They'd taken them.

I sat bolt upright, patting my chest. An ugly sickness crawled through my stomach and my throat became an acid highway. I really wanted to barf, but all I had left was bile. Still needed to take a shite, though.

My eyes snapped into focus. No guard by the exit. There was, however, one on his back by the door. Weapon by his side. Snooze perched on top of his chest. A Cheshire cat grin on his face. His claws kneaded the guards chest like a baker delicately working dough. Clamped to the guard's neck was Finnegan. My cat lay on the floor, his head and teeth attached to what looked like the guard's jugular. A small stream of blood trickled down the guard's neck and formed a small pool by his head. I should've been more surprised by the sight. But I wasn't.

I jumped from the table and wobbled over to my cats. My head pulsed. I felt like I might pass out. The drug still in my system. I knelt by the guard's body and waited for the dizziness to pull away a little. When I opened my eyes, Snooze was right in my face. He pressed his head against mine and purred like the whole world wasn't insane, and I should offer him some tuna. He left a saliva trail along my cheek, marking me. "I love you too, buddy."

I glanced up to Finnegan, still attached to the guard's neck. At first I thought my cat might be dead, his eyes were closed so tight. He seemed so still. I couldn't see a rise or fall of breath. But one of his eyes opened, edged sideways and looked at me. Finnegan didn't appear to be sucking blood from the guards neck, but he remained clamped to the neck.

Snooze turned slightly to Finnegan and then back to me. "Ssslleeepy."

"You're sleepy?"

Snooze kneaded the guards stomach again, pulling on the uniform with his sharp claws. "Ssslleepppy. Heesss ssllepppy."

"He's just asleep?"

As if in answer Finnegan eased away from the guard's throat. I could see four puncture wounds in the guard's neck, above and below, blood dribbling from the wounds, the perfect cat fang size. Finnegan must've bitten deep enough to cause the guard to collapse, and he kept the pressure going just in case. My cats are feckin smart. Despite the blood trickling from the wound, there didn't look to be any permanent damage. "He's gonna wake and feel like a complete twat."

Finnegan and Snooze agreed.

I needed to find my wife and our neighbour. I told Bridget I'd come for her like Daniel Day feckin Lewis. I promised.

I snatched up the guard's weapon. I guessed a semi-automatic. Guessed being the operative word. At least I knew where to find the trigger. "How about we go find mommy and your brother and sister?" I held the weapon muzzle down and started for the door. The gun went off, spraying a quick burst across the floor, and across the guard's legs, sending little spurts of blood popping from his shins. The kick from the gun almost took my arm off. Finnegan and Snooze, thankfully, were not in the line of fire. The guard's legs. . . I'd hit him below the knee, above the ankle. My finger came away from the trigger. "Fuck! My bad." I did feel bad. But that fucker would've shot us given the order. Still, I felt shitty. Somewhere these fuckers had families. I have no doubt. But I'm telling the story, so they're all one dimensional fuckwipes

Only one family occupied my mind. The only family that counted.

I grabbed my coat and we were off.

No, the door wasn't locked.

Chapter

Every corridor looked the same in this feckin place. The facility was a maze. It probably wasn't a maze, but it bloody well felt like one.

I held the gun up in front of me, ready for any surprise, my finger off the trigger. My luck I'd shoot Finnegan or Snooze or my foot.

My two cats ran ahead of me. Every now and then they stopped. Sniffed the air and made that weird face every cat owner knows. Mouth held open, like they'd just smelt a nasty fart. The Flehmen response. The cat sucks air into an organ behind the teeth, getting a sharper olfactory (thank you my thesaurus) image of any interesting odours swirling around. So they're not grimacing when they smell your sweaty socks, they're savoring. There ya go, a little cat anatomy knowledge. Anything more scientific you'll have to go to Wikifuckinpedia.

Finnegan and Snooze were on the hunt for our family, riding along on waves of their scent.

Doors to our left and right. Some contained portal windows so I could stalk up to and peek inside. The base—at least this part—seemed empty.

Finnegan and Snooze halted at a T in the corridor. The fluorescent lights above cast a dull film over everything. My hands looked jaundiced as fuck. The effects of the sedative still clung to my body and every movement came half the normal speed. My stomach felt like crap, and threatened to erupt any second, even though I'd hardly eaten in hours. But the adrenaline pushed me on. I really needed to take a shite. Something you don't see in movies is the hero stopping to take a dump while he searches for the damsel in distress.

I studied my cats as they looked left and right down the T. Even the backs of their heads radiated intelligence. If that's even possible. Finnegan turned to glance up at me. "FFFambbly. Mooommmy." His enunciation was crap. I wasn't able to understand. Where did he cat learn English? Oh, right. Us, and episodes of *Lost*.

Finnegan's stare reached into my head, willing me to understand. His words bounced around my brain and I connected once again with my cat. FFFambbly. Mooommmy. Family. Mommy. Bridget always talked to our cats like they were our children. When she wasn't around, so did I. Cos fellas don't do shite like that. I do, and I feel no shame. Finnegan and Snooze never had the opportunity to hear Bridget call them her babies or say stuff like, "Are ya gonna come up on Mommy's lap?" Finnegan had been around when I dated Bridget, but she rarely came to the house cos our families hated the fuck outta each other. But Leo and Molly did have the opportunity. Wherever they were in this building, our two generations of cats were communicating. Sharing minds.

Family. Mommy.

Somewhere close, our fambly cried out.

Finnegan mewled and headed to the left of the junction. As I moved to follow, Snooze raced off to the right. I froze, not knowing which way to go. I called after Snooze, but at the end of the corridor, he turned another bloody corner, and my orange tabby disappeared. The farther from me he got, the emptier I started to feel. My head clouded. The sensation is hard to explain. Not the drugs this time. Something closer to loss.

Then I felt him reach out, letting me know the connection hadn't broken and he was still there.

An urgent mewl. Finnegan stood at my feet, his tail half up, flicking from side to side, agitated. "FFfaammmily. Wwee's fffightsss." His voice ragged like he smoked three packs a day. His voice developing.

And he was off, racing ahead of me. In my head Finnegan prompted me to follow.

With weapon up, and arse clenched, I followed. I really needed to take a shite.

Chapter

My cat is better than a feckin bloodhound. We trotted all the way to the end of the corridor. Nothing but feckin corridors. Finnegan's nose tasted the air, pulling all the information into his complex arrangement of sensors.

I heard the noise seconds before Finnegan halted at another lab door. His mewls of agitation coursed through my body. His tail flicked back and forth, as he tried to jump to a number combination code box on the wall. I don't know how he hoped to punch in the numbers.

"Heresss, fammbbly!" he hissed as he continued to jump.

Behind the door we heard wails of anger and panic, high pitched and really fuckin pissed off.

Bridget.

"Stand back," I said to Finnegan, and I raised the weapon, ready to let loose—I really was—when the door hissed like Finnegan and opened from inside. Dr. Burke stood in the doorway, looking over his shoulder, head twisted, like the bloody thing might pop off if torqued another fraction. He hadn't noticed me or Finnegan. His lab coat billowed out like wings ready to take flight. Scratch marks etched the side of his face, fresh and bloodied. Behind him I heard chaos and crashing. Metal being thrown. Verbal abuse being hurled. Banshees screaming. Wails of panic. Then the chilling sound of gunfire. I stepped forward, and just as I did, Burke turned and bellied into the muzzle of my gun. His eyes sprang open. Nothing but black empty irises remained. His scream came as shrill as a little girl through his mask.

Finnegan wasted no time. He swiftly slipped by Burke into the room.

I shoved the muzzle deeper into the doctor's gut. "What the fuck did you do to my wife and cats?"

"What did *we* do to *them*?" Burke looked on the verge of tears as he bolted passed me and legged it down the corridor.

I turned back to the room. A glorious sight met me. The tallest doctor, Smythe or whatever the fuck his name was, cowered on the ground beside a metal exam table, the arms of his white uniform torn to shreds. Blood streaked the white coat like splashed paint. The backs of his hands ripped to shreds. His face in tatters. Runnels ripped by claws marked his skin.

On the ground, not two feet away from the doc, Leo crouched, legs splayed, his hair puffed out, back arched, almost doubling his size. His claws pulled on the tiled floor, the clicking sound of nails carried all the way to the doorway. They needed trimming. His body in definite attack mode, primed to spring through the air and tear the lanky fuck apart. His one eye focused sharp. His hiss, scrotum clenching. But in the hiss I heard, "Nooooss." Hiss. "Tooouucch, fammlllyyy." His pronunciation better than Finnegan's. Leo's eyes flicked to me, and they communicated fear, and sadness, and happy to see me, all at once.

Smythe screamed, "No please. No more."

A metal object flew through the air, too fast for me to tell what it was. I heard Doctor Newman scream in pain. In the center of the room, to my right, Newman backed away, hands up, shielding himself from further flying sharp objects. A scalpel was embedded in his forearm. He yanked the scalpel out and threw it to the ground. X-ray sheets lay scattered and dark at his feet. I couldn't make out any images, but I didn't give a toss what they revealed. Bridget stood to the left. Her coat off, the blue dress she'd gotten from the hotel on the floor and she wore one of those hospital gowns where your arse hangs out the back. I never got one of them. Two holes in the fabric exploded outward from her titty region, like Leo and Molly had shot from a cannon. right through the gown. Our two cats taking matters into their own paws, protecting Bridget. Those two had really come out of their shells. Or tits. Anyway, they must've been pissed.

Despite how exposed she looked, Bridget didn't seem to give a shite. She reached to the counter beside her, picked up something metal and sharp, and threw the object (another scalpel maybe) with an uncanny force, like a fuckin warrior woman. Newman dodged and it hit the wall behind him. I could see she'd run out of shit to throw. She resorted to the old reliable. "Touch me or me cats again and I'll feckin burst ya." Or "Ya fuckin cunt ya!" Or "Ya fuckin fuck!" One of my favorites. Maybe a combination of all three. She pulled a hand sanitizer dispenser from the wall and hurled that with equal vigor.

Where was Molly?

I heard the scream first and imagined one of my cats being hit. At the back of the lab, another soldier (sorry, they all looked the same), staggered backward, Molly attached to his face, and Finnegan attached to his weapon arm, biting into the skin, using the same pressure he'd used on our guard's neck. I don't know, I'm only guessing. The soldier yelled at the top of his lungs, competing with the piercing cries of Molly. "Get them off me! Get them off me," he screamed. Or something along those lines. Molly's body consumed the guard's face like a hairy Alien facehugger. The man swung from side to side but Molly and Finnegan clung on. The soldier swung the gun around, Finnegan going along for the ride. The spray of bullets opened up the floor at his feet, hitting no one.

Finnegan bit deeper. The guard lowered the weapon to the floor, his hand pumping blood. Nevertheless, he attempted to pull Molly free of his face with his other hand. Molly's claws tore away the back of the soldier's head and she sank her fangs into his skin. I think I even heard her teeth hit the bone, but I could be wrong. The surge of noise and chaos around me played tricks and danced in my ears. Molly lifted her kitty head and hissed," Nnnooo huuurnt fffamily." Her voice sang high, cutting the air.

The guard managed to tear Molly from his face, but her claws left long scars on his cheeks. He flung Molly across the lab. My heart stopped. But in mid air, Molly twisted her body, righted herself, and practically landed in the lap of that poxy shite, Smythe, who still cowered on the floor near Leo. Molly and Leo were back as a team.

Finnegan took advantage of the moment. The frazzled guard attempted to shake away the confusion, his skull cap visible and glistening in the crappy lab light. Finnegan bit again into the soldier's trigger hand. The guard screamed and the weapon finally dropped to the floor, Finnegan right behind. The guard made an attempt to both care for his bloodied hand and reach for his gun. Finnegan pounced and clamped around his forearm, penetrating the material of his uniform. More blood. The guard swung my cat from his arm, but Finnegan landed on his feet. The poor bastard didn't have a chance to either run or retrieve his gun. In a single, graceful bound, Finnegan latched onto the jugular.

Meanwhile, Leo and Molly crouched, their bold muscles tense and ready. Smythe kicked his legs out. Attempted to scoot back on his arse, but his head hit the metal exam table. In a moment of communication, which I heard somewhere in my head, in an area where I connected to our cats, I heard Leo say, and I quote, "Let's do this bastard."

A perfect sentence structure. No hiss, or half formed language garbled with cat. That's what it sounded like at the time.

"Yes," Molly replied, not in my head. Her voice radiated through the lab. Molly and Leo, brother and sister, leapt at Smythe. Despite the obstacle behind, he edged backward, his hands up. Hands were useless. Leo went for his nuts, and Molly went for the neck.

"Get mommy," echoed through my head, in Leo's voice. His pronunciation definitely improving.

So I did.

Bridget raged like a feckin fire. I'd never seen her as angry and as passionate. In an instant, cos all what just happened, happened really bloody quick, I leapt to my wife's side. Bridget's whole body, grounded and sharpened, was focused on protecting itself, fighting back. I grabbed her arm. She swung for me. I managed to duck. Her arm came back again, but she froze. Recognized me. Her steel face softened, and she pulled me into her arms. We should've done one of those big kisses Hollywood expects, but she stank of sweat and we both had horrible breath. She did pull me close and I felt her head against my head and felt the fire and anger pulse between our bodies and I drew from that. I felt powerful. We felt powerful. Forget Beyonce and whatever his fuckin name is, we were the new power couple.

Newman darted for the door. Finnegan bolted after him, but as Newman crossed the threshold, the lab door slammed in Finnegan's face, locking us in.

Bridget glanced at the weapon in my hand and a light came to her eyes, the same mischievous and randy light I remember as a teenager when we first met. I so wanted to get her into the back of a car.

Finnegan's disarmed soldier lay slumped and bloodied against the wall at the back of the lab. Hard to believe the damage created by one cat. He protected us. Our cat protected us from harm.

The sight of the blood made me slightly queasy. We hadn't eaten in a long stretch and I felt both sick and famished simultaneously. My head swung back to the emptiness I felt when Snooze disappeared a few minutes ago. Not complete emptiness. We still held a thin wire connection.

Bridget grabbed my face in her sausage fingers and planted a dry, but passionate kiss on my lips. Hollywood kiss? Her lips were chapped, but I gave in to their frantic appeal and need. Her breath smelled a little like a cat's arse, but given the circumstances, I welcomed her lips. We pulled apart, but our eyes stayed locked. The reach as intimate as I've ever experienced.

At our feet, three cats, Molly, Leo, and Finnegan stared up. Finnegan spoke first. "Go now?"

Honestly, I didn't bother checking on the soldier for signs of life. Smythe lay on the ground, curled in a fetal position, holding his bloody ball bag. Not my concern. My concern was family.

Bridget pulled on the blue dress. She looked good. Then the Da's coat (which smelled a little better now). She popped on her shoes, and we made for the door.

Locked.

Bridget shot me a concerned look. "What do we do?"

"Like in the movies when the heroes don't have a key to the doors." I stood back and let the weapon loose on the code box to the door's left. Sparks flew and shells fell like me old man's teeth after asking one of his equally drunk mates to punch him in the face cos he couldn't feel his cheeks anymore. His mate obliged. True story. The Da got fifteen free pints, but lost most of his teeth. I sat on a bar stool as his stained, yellow teeth, now coated with blood, fell to the floor of the pub, and everyone cheered. Good times.

The bullets obliterated the box. I pushed on the door. It opened no problem. I presented Bridget with a shit eating grin. Now I did feel like Daniel Day Lewis. Even though I still hated the bastard. Smythe on the floor. The soldier slumped against the back wall. Neither moved. Down their chests, the blood, dark and red, as if they'd just eaten a kebab. My stomach raised the issue of hunger. And I still needed a shite. I pushed the urges down. We needed to get outta here. Find Gemma.

We stepped through to the corridor.

The alarms started roaring through the facility.

That actually took longer than I expected.

Chapter

The moment we crossed into the corridor, soldiers with even bigger guns than the last batch greeted us. Bigger guns, and more soldiers. They weren't taking any chances with these vicious nipple cats, or titty kitties. I knew at some stage we'd have to ask our felines which name they preferred.

Our escape blocked, left and right. The soldiers looked pissed off. But most looked scared.

Good.

"Drop the weapon." Dr. Newman sliced his way through the soldiers. His arms bloodied where Bridget managed to hit flesh with scalpels. The red looked great against the white. "There's nowhere you can run." His voice no longer the curious doctor, and more the mad fucker than the mad scientist.

My finger inched toward the trigger. But I knew I couldn't pull on the soldiers. We wouldn't stand a chance. Like the end of *Butch Cassidy,* only we wouldn't freeze-frame forever on a screen.

Finnegan clawed his way up my thigh, which hurt cos he managed to snag my sack on the way, but I absorbed the pain and didn't flinch. The soldiers followed his progress up my body with their weapons.

Two soldiers brushed past us and entered the lab. Next second we heard, "Jaysus t'fuck. It's a massacre here, Sarge."

A larger officer with a handgun—Sarge, I assumed, but couldn't see any stripes—stepped past us, one eye on me, one on our cats. And I mean they worked independently of each other. He took a quick look inside. "Anyone alive?"

"The doc looks like his balls've been pulled apart, Sarge."

"Anyone else? What about Gorman?" Uh oh, the soldier had a name.

"Looking for signs now, Sarge."

Sarge waited.

Newman looked pissed. "Drop the fucking weapon."

You always know when people in Ireland are serious when they remember to pronounce the 'g' at the end of their words.

"Or what? You'll shoot us?" I said. My best Bruce Willis voice this time. Much better choice than Daniel Day fuckin Lewis. I like Bruce Willis. I should've used one of his quotes earlier. "I don't think so." I leveled the gun at Bridget, then our cats. Bridget's eyes popped open. Inside my coat Finnegan burrowed back into me tit. I could feel him shifting. No purr now. I wanted the purrs back.

"You wouldn't shoot," Newman said, though his voice registered a tinge of fear.

"To stop you messin around with my wife's tits and our cats? Absolutely I would." In that moment I wasn't lying. I would do it. Turn the gun on myself. Why not? Perfect end to a fucked up day. Leo, Molly, Finnegan, and wherever Snooze was, would leg it outta here to safety. That's if they didn't die with us. Or, maybe when we died, they died. Like we both depended on each other to live. I kinda liked the idea.

"Get some medics in here," the Sarge yelled. "They're actually alive."

"Shite," I said. "Better luck next time."

"There won't be a next time," Newman pointed to the soldiers around him. "You may get off a few shots. Maybe kill your wife there. . ." I snatched a quick look at Bridget. Leo and Molly, down by Bridget's feet hissed at Newman. Leo let loose a barrage of curses. Honestly I don't know where he got the language from. Oh, wait. . . us again. We probably also watched way too much British tele. The barrage of "Fucckkkerrsss," and "Cunttsss," confused the fuck outta the soldiers.

"But we would mow you down without compunction," Newman went on ignoring the insults. "Men, if he even looks ready to pull the trigger, take his legs out from underneath him."

Fuck!

Newman pointed at Molly and Leo. "Then shoot the little furry fuckers."

Bridget let out a pained squeak. Molly and Leo hissed again. Ran up Bridget's leg, and scrambled into the coat, and into her titties. Guns followed their every move.

Newman looked really pissed off, and looked like he'd follow through with full scale slaughter. Behind Newman I saw Dr. Burke, his face looked a shredded mess despite the freshly applied plasters and stuff. He looked scared.

Good.

"Leave me the fuck alone." The voice came from behind the crowd of soldiers. A gap parted and Gemma stumbled through. In her arms she carried Snooze.

Gemma noticed us and rushed to our side. "Thank god you're all okay. They do anything to you?"

"They tried." Bridget snapped a smug look at Newman. The doctor didn't take the slight very well.

"What about you?" I asked.

"It's all good. Dublin bitches are harder than they look."

Another shared look with my wife. "I know that."

We hadn't made this much eye contact in forfuckingever.

Gemma jerked her head in the direction she'd just come, over the heads of the soldiers. "Snooze found me. Took out the guard. We were just about to leg it. . ."

Snooze jumped from Gemma's arms onto my shoulder. He arched his back in a stretch and rubbed his head against my balding scalp. Then crawled down to my chest and inched inside me and huddled with Finnegan, his adopted brother. There's something about having your first cat, your childhood feline, always a part of you somewhere. I felt complete and in my head begged him never to leave me. Because I knew in that moment, I would lose a chunk of my being if we were separated again. Pretty deep for a Dublin twat like meself, huh?

"I want to see how everything works in there," Newman said, pointing at us like we were specimens. "But not here. I want to take you to my underground bunker, ah, lab in Germany. I have more of what I need on hand."

"I fuckin knew ya were German," I blurted. "Ya Nazi bastard."

"Grandfathers have such knowledge to share." He followed that with a villainous grin.

"How the fuck did a Nazi get into Ireland?" Gemma asked.

Newman smiled smugly. "After the war, your country practically invited Nazis in, giving some of our best practitioners asylum, and a new life. Wanted the knowledge we carried."

The last few days. . . insane. Absolutely insane. Last thing I expected? Nazis. If leprechauns riding the souls of Irish rebels arrived to save the day, I wouldn't have batted an eye.

"I want to explore your condition further. But I would be quite happy killing one of you and letting the other watch. I just need one person. You. . ." He pointed at me. "Or you." To Bridget.

"What about me?" Gemma asked.

"You have no role in my work," Newman hardly looked at her. "You'll disappear."

The soldiers stood frozen. None seemed to acknowledge the orders they'd been given.

"Well I choose Barbados," Gemma said.

"What?" Newman looked way over this shite.

"If I'm gonna disappear, then I want somewhere sunny, not this miserable fuckin country."

"I don't think so. Maybe a field behind the compound if you are lucky."

"Fuck you, ya little midget sheep fucker." Gemma smiled proudly. Happy with her insult. She leaned into my ear a whispered, "I found a phone charger." No one had taken her phone. And some twat left a phone charger lying around?

"What's it going to be?" asked Newman, like I made the decisions in our gaff. "Shoot one of you, so your spouse sees you die. Or just come with us on a little trip. I promise, when the time comes. . . you'll be taken care of. . . respectfully."

"Seeing as you're the grandson of a Nazi. . . ," I said, "I'll take your word for it. Fuckin arsehole."

I dropped the weapon.

What the fuck else could I've done?

Chapter

Two gurneys arrived before we moved and scooped up Dr. Smythe and the soldier Finnegan had mutilated, and whisked them away. Smythe moaned, clutching his nads, whining on about his balls being really, really painful. Granted, there was a lot of blood.

On the move. Another corridor. Here the fluorescent lights flickered and crackled like rashers in a pan. Totally fuckin bollixed, they were. My vision strobed, and I swear any second I'd go epileptic. Some people can go epo with strobe lights.

Ahead, Newman goose stepped (He didn't. But, ya know. . .) protected by two soldiers. More flanked us. They weren't taking any chances.

In my head, communication snapped back and forth, as all four of our kitties set plans in motion. Bridget heard the same. She looked at me and nodded. In my head I heard her voice: "Do you hear them?" I answered, "Yes," and that's all we needed. The family had plans. I could feel the rising in my body and on the air. Bridget felt it, and she pressed in closer. No fuckin way anyone was gonna lay a hand our kitties.

Flicker, crackle.

On my left, Gemma tapped my leg. I looked down, and what the fuck do you know? Her mobile hung in her hand by her side. I couldn't tell if she just had audio or if she was recording the whole thing.

Flicker, crackle.

Footsteps on tile.

Flicker, crackle.

Body tensed.

Flicker, crackle.

Snooze and Finnegan snuck from my tits, from the coat, and onto my shoulders. . . then sprang. Their movements unnatural in the flashing of the failing lights as they leapt from my shoulder to the floor. Barely touched ground. In a liquid motion, fast as anything I've ever seen, my two cats sprang from the floor.

Screaming like banshees.

In the next instant, Leo and Molly were in the air like cats with rabies, hissing and spitting, saliva flying, as they glided onto the face of another soldier. The soldier wailed, as he spun, his weapon in the air, firing wildly, cutting into the ceiling, knocking out some of the fluorescent lighting in a shower of sparks.

We all ducked. Gemma against the wall. I pulled Bridget to my side.

Leo gripped the top of a soldier's skull, and bunny kicked with his powerful hind legs raking the soldier's face to minced meat.

Finnegan raced up one soldier's legs and onto his nuts, digging deep, and dragging himself all the way up the soldier's body. The man dropped to his knees clutching his crotch, dropped his weapon, and screamed at a pitch only dogs could hear.

In the same moment, Snooze glided through the air like one of those tree squirrels and attached himself to Newman's back. Sinking his claws deep into his spine. Newman went down screaming like an air raid siren, attempting pathetically to pull Snooze from his back. Snooze's heart raced (I could still feel him inside me) with fear and excitement, as he scrambled up the doctor's back, riding Newman to his knees. Snooze pulled himself over the top of the doctor's head and started to bite and claw at the doctor's face. Bunny kicks again. Newman's hands worked to pull my cat's razor claws from his, "Mein eyes!"

Somewhere behind, Dr. Burke screamed like a little kid and ran in the opposite direction.

Soldiers turned their weapons on anything that moved. I stepped back, grabbed Bridget and Gemma and pulled them away from the mess.

In all the chaos, I could detect, individually, all our cats, just by sounds. Finnegan with his brave growl, deep and throaty like Charles Bronson. Snooze, his scream higher, mixed with fear and excitement, a Celtic warrior in battle. Leo, spitting as he attacked and cut with claws and teeth, simultaneously laughing and purring, as if he'd found his true joy in life. His voice spat, "Protecttt," the 't' like a whip at the end of the spit. And Molly, like my Bridget, not a hesitation in her opera singer cry. Our cats communicated as they attacked. Strategizing. There came a moment, where all our cats, in coordination, like a collective brain, bunny kicked faces and necks of all those who wanted us harmed. Imagine the scene. In slow motion. Spirals of smoke. Soldiers twisting. Balls of fur and rage adhered to their heads.

Gun fire. Sparks of light.

I pulled the girls away from the battle. Bridget fought me, wanting to go and help our kitties.

The sound of more screaming. Cat and soldier.

Then the gut churning yowl of a cat in pain.

The slow motion froze. Real time kicked back in. Reality hit us. And tears followed.

Chapter

The gunfire echoed in a chaotic peel of sound and light.

Bridget wrenched herself from me and ran back into the violence. Fuckin women.

I ran after her. Two soldiers on the ground, covered their faces as Molly ripped away at one of the soldier's cheeks, still kicking. The soldier no longer held his gun, instead he used his hands to protect his face. Pointless as Molly ripped the skin off the backs of his hands.

The other soldier still held onto his gun and pulled himself up from the floor. Bridget swung her leg as she passed, and with a rage and the full force of a pissed off woman behind her, yelled mournfully, at a pitch which broke my heart. And drove her foot up between the soldier's legs. I swear I heard his nuts pop.

Bridget dropped to her knees, and held the limp body of Leo, the back half of his body, which minutes before curled inside her, hung, torn apart and dripping blood.

Gemma took advantage of the moment. I saw her alternatively kick a grounded soldier in the back and face. Then record everything, like a war journalist in Kosovo or somewhere in Ballymun. Finnegan and Snooze darted back and forth between the other soldiers, ripping off pieces of any exposed flesh they could find. Most of the military escort lay on the ground. Including Sarge, who clutched both his buttocks and crotch. His radio beside him on the ground. Useless, unless he took one of his hands away from the wounds.

Newman had disappeared.

We needed to move.

I dropped to my knees beside Bridget. She turned, tears gushing from her eyes, and presented to me the damaged body of Leo. She pressed Leo to her chest and bowed her head.

Gemma beside me. "We have to get the fuck outta here."

Molly, no longer attacking the soldier, jumped into Bridget's arms, sniffed her brother and wailed. "Gonesss! Awaysss!"

I wanted to curl up and die. I wanted our bed at home, where all the chaos could fall away into an ignorant sleep; where we would never wake again. The home and beds we left that morning, would never be ours again.

Finnegan, Snooze, and Molly. . . we needed to take them to safety.

I touched Bridget's shoulder, and pulled her arm. She wouldn't budge. Her chest splotched with blood from where Leo's body rested in her arms. Molly pressed her head into Bridget's chest. "We have to go," I said, more a whisper. She turned to me. Soldiers moaned but were finding their senses. Bridget found her maternal instincts and stood, Leo still in her arms. Molly jumped down. Her eyes never left her brother's body. I pulled Bridget, and this time she moved.

Chapter

Finnegan and Snooze raced ahead of us. Gemma, me, Bridget, and Molly followed. We trusted the direction our cats were taking us. Why the fuck we did that, I have no rational idea. But so far. . .

At a T break in the corridor, Finnegan, Snooze and Molly stopped. All three cats brushed heads. Communicating with scent and sound. "Thisss wayss familiesss," said Finnegan. The three cats turned to the left, sniffed the air, and took off in that direction.

As we headed to freedom, we heard the calls of the doctors, the soldiers. The whole world it sounded like. No one behind us for now. I regretted the many fish and chip dinners and all the pints I'd guzzled. So much feckin beer. I wasn't in shape to run. My breathing hurt.

A new alarm peeled through the facility, but no signs of a mighty military force attempting to block us.

The door ahead didn't look very high security. Finnegan and Snooze looked wired and focused as we caught up with them by the door. Both cats were alert, tails puffed, ears flat and back, eyes bulging from their sockets. Finnegan tried to push against the door with his body. He was always a smart cat, and he knew generally how doors worked. As a kitten, to get into the back kitchen in our house he'd stand on the counter, push his weight down on the door's handle until it popped the door slightly. Then he'd jump down and force the door the rest of the way. From there he proceeded to raid the fridge by catching his claw just under the rubber seal and pulling. We lost a lot of cheese and sliced ham that way.

I didn't wait for Gemma and Bridget to catch up. I slammed my body against the pressure bar on the door and we all broke out into the darkness and the rain. Finnegan and Snooze's fur slicked with the beating downpour, but they kept running into the night. Behind me Gemma and Bridget came through the door. Bridget still cradled the body of Leo in one arm. Molly wailed like the alarm siren behind us, but her wails cut deep and pain welled from somewhere inside her guts.

I kept running, but made sure Bridget and Gemma were right behind me.

"Over there!" Gemma's call sliced through the sounds behind me and I stopped dead. Turned. Gemma pointed to the side of the large facility we'd exited and I saw the Humvee.

Finnegan and Snooze both halted, glanced over their shoulders, getting their bearings. "Boys," I called. "This way." They didn't move. They stood and sniffed the air through the rain. I approached them. Both my boys rubbed against my legs, in and around, a figure eight.

"Sssoon," Finnegan said.

Snooze held his body against my legs. I ran my hand down his back until his arse elevated. "Seesss again. Sssoooon," he purred out.

Then both of my beloved cats darted off into the night.

I stood for a moment, paralyzed. "Don't go."

But I knew I was too late. They were already gone. And my tears washed with the rain.

I started when a hand touched my shoulder. Bridget, with Molly and Leo. "Gemma is getting the truck."

She called everything bigger than a Toyota Corolla, a truck.

From somewhere else on the grounds, I could hear voices calling and shouting. "I see two of those bloody animals. Over here." The fuckers found Snooze and Finnegan.

I wanted to run to them. My fuckin cats were using themselves as distractions. Somehow I knew they would get away, but they would be lost. How would they live, survive out there, wherever? They were certainly exceptional animals, so they'd find a way.

The Humvee roared up beside Gemma and me. The doors flew open. "Get the fuck in," Gemma yelled. "I'm just tryin to figure out how to drive one of these big fuckers."

Bridget hopped in the back with Leo and Molly. I pulled myself from my thoughts and I followed by jumping into the passenger seat and reefed the door closed. Gemma looked confused. "Where are the boys?"

"They're helping us escape," I said. My stomach ached with a sick pain of loss. The kind of sickness where the wave of sadness overwhelms you and your eyes fill with water and your nose clogs with snot and you feel empty and nothing you do will pull your mind away from thinking about how your cats are suffering. Because you see their fear and pain. "So just go, please."

Bridget's hand rested on my shoulder. Molly climbed up Bridget's arm and jumped into my lap and curled up, her head pressing into the crook of my arm and I hugged her tight.

Bridget never took her hand from my shoulder. I felt a light pressure on my skin and the small weight in my lap.

But I knew Finnegan and Snooze were no longer near. My eyes fogged over and as much as I wanted, I couldn't stay focused on the present. The same sensation I'd felt when Snooze left me in the corridor poured through my body and out my eyeballs. But more encompassing. I slipped slowly from reality. You fuckin laugh. All I know is, the farther we got from Finnegan and Snooze, the more I disconnected from the world. In their loss I felt lost.

Behind us, two Humvees raced through the muck and the dark, distorted by our rear lights bouncing like. . . I don't know, lightsabers? Gemma can really drive her arse off. Our Humvee fishtailed and slid over the rain drenched fields. Gemma eased up on the accelerator. The other two Humvees came up on our right and left. All I saw were lights in blurs as we bumped and rocked. Wipers swiped rain back and forth.

"Holy fuck, where'd you learn to drive?" My voice sounded foreign and detached.

Gemma never took her eyes off the darkness ahead of us, and said, "Shut up. Concentratin."

In my lap Molly dug her claws into my leg, but she purred against my chest. In my head her vibrations told me to stay calm.

Humvee beside me. To the left. By my window. They were close. If they pulled in front of us. . .

In an instant my mind cleared, the fog retreated. Finnegan and Snooze were close. I turned to the passenger window. The Humvee. The driver. And that Nazi fuck, Newman. The wanker sat behind the driver, pointing like a spastic out the window at us. He looked like he was saluting. Gobshite. Then, just before the Humvee jerked away from us, I saw the driver reach for his head. In that moment I saw Snooze, my orange tabby racking bunny kicks across the driver's face. Newman screamed in blind panic. He glanced at me one last time, his face jumping from angry to scared shitless, his fate set in stone. The Humvee jerked away, like it suddenly remembered it left the iron on, and disappeared into the night. To the right, on Gemma's side, the other pursuer weaved toward us. Gemma yanked on the wheel and pulled away. The Humvee didn't slide in our direction again. The last Humvee bastard also looked way out of control. Through the driver's side window, I just made out Finnegan's furry body attached to the driver's face like a limpet. Blood slashed across the driver's window. Then the Humvee disappeared into the night. I heard Finnegan's and Snooze's growls fill my senses for one more moment.

And then they were gone. Like air sucked from a room.

Silence filled the car. The loss came again. Finnegan and Snooze were no longer in my head.

Chapter

I sit on the small stone doorstep of the cottage and look out over the lake and the mountains. Bridget steps out of the darkness behind me and I shuffle my arse over to give her room. She hands me a steaming cup of tea. The landscape is covered in a mist and the rain just stopped about ten minutes ago. Not far from where we sit a small hill holds a marker where we piled up some of the rocks we found down by the shore of the lake. Leo lies beneath the rocks, so he's there when we look out the door or the window.

Molly races up from the shore, and comes to a trot, her tail in the air, curled into a question mark. She climbs the small hill and sits down by her brother's marker and stares out at the isolated landscape, keeping him company. Then she licks her arse. Cats.

Snooze and Finnegan. They just disappeared into the rain, taking those bastardin soldiers and mad doctor with them. I really fucking miss them. The cats not the soldiers.

My head doesn't feel as lost now. My wife and our remaining kitty have healed me. I believe that with all my heart and my soul. Sappy shite again.

How'd we get here? I'll tell ya what my wife told me, cos honestly, most of the journey's a big feckin blank to me.

After the high-speed car chase, there were helicopters, explosions, and fist fights. That's what Bridget told me. Then she said, "I'm just taken the mickey." I like we can joke again. She also let me know I'd taken that shite I'd desperately needed while we raced away in the Humvee. All over me pants. Bridget eventually cleaned me up. Wouldn't take any help from Gemma. That's the first time she's ever had to wipe my arse. I love her more for that than any ride she's ever given me. Though, she says if she ever has to wipe me hole again, it's divorce. And I know she's not taking the mickey about that.

Bridget recounted the events. We drove the Humvee across more fields, through an electric fence, narrowly avoided a bunch of cows and sheep. Made it to an old farmhouse. Just as helicopters neared in the distance. We were in Wicklow, not far from Dublin. An old couple saw the Humvee and were initially freaked the fuck out, but they recognized Gemma from the news, and Bridget and Gemma told our whole story. They believed them when Molly popped out of Bridget's tits and asked for some food. The old couple almost keeled over with shock. But when they'd recovered, they both played with Molly and a piece of string as we ate (I was hand fed, cos I still wasn't aware of much). If they'd only seen the bloody chaos our titty kitties were capable of. . .

Gemma, with her newly charged mobile, called Marcus, our old neighbour, and he came out and picked us up. Again, I remember little in my shutdown state, just vague snippets, as I drifted through a haze of shock and pain. I was told, at night, Molly insisted on curling up in the crook of my arm, purring, and muttering, "Sssad, ssssad," over and over. I kinda remember that.

Marcus felt like shite about the way we were treated by the media and our neighbours, and agreed to drive us wherever we wanted. Gemma showed him the evidence of our ordeal on her mobile and he was appalled.

Gemma, our official manager and agent now, negotiated so much in our bloody favor, and from so many outlets across the globe, she amassed us a small fortune. And her twenty percent. We upped that to twenty-five percent. She's family now, like it or not. Marcus, with a little financial finesse, found a sneaky way to filter our money out of the country, just in case the authorities came after us. But our images never went up on the news as "Wanted," and the Gardai never issued a "be on the lookout." We became the victims, not the freaks.

Gemma has continued documenting our story, letting people all over the world know our titty kitties are real and not Jim Henson puppets. No mad Nazi scientists have been found, by the way. Maybe Newman is six feet under or still in Ireland somewhere. Bastard.

There are movie offers, book offers, and even a children's book called *Explore the World with the Titty Kitties* in the works. Talk about a whirl fuckin wind. News and fads travel at the speed of fuckin light and sound.

Sounds. I remember the sound of water and waves. The feel of a sharp wind on my face. We arrived at the island on a "small" boat which Marcus owned. "Small" my arse. The thing had two rooms and a jax. Rich fucker. But fair play to him.

Where were we? An island. Somewhere off the coast of Scotland. Where it gets feckin colder than a witch's tit.

Two weeks ago, the cloud lifted and I slowly came back to the world. Mostly. Finnegan and Snooze's tit holes haven't healed. I remember, half awake, the sensation of Bridget hugging the crap outta me. "My Daniel Day Lewis," she said, tears in her eyes.

Daniel Day Feckin Lewis. For fucksake.

As for Finnegan and Snooze? Not a word. I think about my two titty kitties out there in the cold and the damp and the rain of Ireland. Fending for themselves. I'm back in the world, but my two boys are no longer connected to me.

After a cup of tea, and a few rubs and kisses from Molly, Bridget filled me in on the last part of our mad journey. After, we took a walk around the island, hand in hand, the silence broken only by Molly's harsh language as she playful attempted to capture a resident falcon. We are healing slowly.

Gemma took our story into the world. News footage, interviews, the lot. The mobile footage verified authentic. Up yours, Nazi bastards! You're not gonna weaponize my titty kitties. No word on Dr. Newman. Hopefully Finnegan took care of him on that Humvee ride.

No one knows our location. No hassle from the media, or anyone else. The world has started to believe. We still have to hide the fuck away, though. Maybe there's more folks like us out there. People with pets popping from their bodies. I hope there are, and I hope there aren't.

Molly rubs against her brother's burial marker and trots up to us on the doorstep. She stops to lick her behind for a few seconds. Finished with her anal scrubbing, she proceeds to hack up a hairball. She recovers quickly, then bumps her head lovingly against my leg. Bridget opens her shirt and exposes her titties. They are full and beautiful. And I love 'em. Molly climbs up Bridget's stomach and pushes her way into my wife's tits and disappears. Bridget giggles like it tickles. A second later, Molly's head and paws appear once again and our cat smiles, her eyes closed in contentment, a deep purr rumbling through her and into our tranquil bodies. "Homess. Wesss homess," she says.

Yes. Home. Not all of us. But yes, we home.

Chapter

Bridget and I lie in the same bed, face to face. Teeth brushed first. Holding hands. Molly sleeps between us, resting half on my body and half on Bridget's. Bridging us.

We both jerk awake at the same time, startling each other. Confused. "Did I fart again?" I ask.

But we both feel the sensations at the same time. And we both begin to cry.

The first furry head appears from my left titty.

"Snooze!"

GARVAN GILTINAN is a recovering Irishman with a fascination for the bizarre/grotesque/puerile. His work has appeared in anthologies *New England: Weird Triggered*, *Fatal Fetish*, *Unsplatterpunk*, and the *Anthology of Bizarro* from HellBound Books. His novel *Backdoor Carnivore* will be published by JEA Press in 2020. He has an MFA in Creative Writing and really weirds his wife and cats out with the subject matter of his stories.

www.ingramcontent.com/pod-product-compliance
Lightning Source LLC
Chambersburg PA
CBHW051924110726
47902CB00002B/411